Get hooked on Victoria Houston's
Loon Lake Fishing Mysteries . . .

Dead Hot Mama

"Enough to make anyone long for the scent of pines. An addictive series . . . A complicated mystery with plenty of red herrings (and a few muskies) . . . that will have readers guessing up until the last minute. Another strong entry into a very atmospheric and entertaining series that will have even the most sun-worshipping readers consider digging a hole in the ice, dropping a line in, and hoping for a bite." —*The Mystery Reader*

Dead Frenzy

"Houston has a way with words . . . Her humor is well-rationed . . . The good doctor is a pleasant, witty voice. The description of a fishing experience is well-done, depicting the Northwoods to a 'T.' The mystery is plotted well, and there is enough action to keep the reader engaged to the end. The Loon Lake series holds great promise for a pleasurable reading retreat." —*Books 'n' Bytes*

Dead Water

"*Dead Water* is her best yet . . . [Victoria Houston] puts me right there in the Wisconsin heat and cold, lets me know what the fish are biting on, lets me spy on the interesting characters of Loon Lake, and most of all, spins an intelligent and captivating tale. I look forward to more and more." —T. Jefferson Parker, author of *California Girl*

"Victoria Houston's love for her Wisconsin setting—and her wonderful characters—is evident on every page of her fine series . . . A great getaway, even if it does keep me up at nights." —Laura Lippman, author of *To the Power of Three*

continued . . .

"As exciting as fishing a tournament—and you don't know the result until the end."   —Norb Wallock,
    North American Walleye Angler's 1997 Angler of the Year

"Houston introduces us to a cast of characters with whom we quickly bond—as fly fishers and as good citizens—in the first of what I hope will be a long series."
                              —Joan Wulff, world-class fly caster
                   and cofounder of the Wulff School of Fly Fishing

"A compelling thriller . . . populated with three-dimensional characters who reveal some of their secrets of trout fishing the dark waters of the northern forests."
                         —Tom Wiench, dedicated fly-fisherman
                                  and member of Trout Unlimited

"Should net lots of fans—a good catch."
                                  —*The Muncie (IN) Star Press*

"Colorful and eccentric characters . . . Readers who prefer their fish either in a restaurant or supermarket exclusively will still enjoy this delightful mystery because Victoria Houston hooks her audience from start to finish. The Great Lakes make a wonderful backdrop to fine characters and a delightful storyline . . . This regional mystery has a powerful (somewhat fishy) taste to it."   —*Midwest Book Review*

one

All freezes again—
Among the pines, winds
Whispering a prayer.

—Riei, eighteenth-century Japanese poet

The eagle ate well that day. When Brian's truck rattled over the hill and, tires squealing, shuddered through a skid, the flurry of action forced the bird into the air—but only fifty feet. Refusing to be intimidated, the eagle lurked high in a nearby tree, convinced he could frighten the intruder away with a rustle of magnificent wings, a stare from a malevolent eye. He would not give up such a kill so easily.

But the man climbing out of the green Forest Service truck had so much on his mind that he barely noticed. Just one more eagle feasting on carrion. No, Brian Jensen's concern was the overturned car. He couldn't keep going with a clear conscience unless he was sure no one was trapped inside.

The sight of the vehicle in the ditch stumped him. Other than bird hunters, few people traveled this stretch of condemned road. He'd started using it after a recent field project, during which he'd stumbled onto a shortcut home. He could drive the dead highway to where it intersected a logging trail. After a bumpy two miles, the trail connected to a farmer's driveway that opened onto County A—just three miles short of his house. Cut fifteen minutes from his drive home.

Even so, he used it only when he was running late and seldom when driving his own car. The loose gravel was treacherous under wheels, not to mention that one stone could crack a windshield and ruin his insurance premium. He was driving it today because the monthly staff meeting had run on way too long. He was due to leave on his vacation at noon—it was already past one. His wife would not be happy.

Catching sight of the metal and glass flashing in the sun, his first instinct was to keep going. But he knew better than that. He might be off duty, but he was still in the Forest Service, a public servant. He could check it out, call in the location on his car phone, and leave a message for one of his colleagues to follow up. It would take five minutes, max.

Brian pulled the truck over and opened the door, leaving the engine idling. He jogged toward the ditch and the overturned car, the shrill of grasshoppers pulsing in the August heat. As he approached the car, he could see it was a powder blue Chrysler Sebring convertible and that it had rolled with its top down. Ouch. A sudden breeze carried a whiff of bad air. And it wasn't the smell of gas.

He paused to listen . . . no sound—just grasshoppers and the low hum of his truck.

Brian walked the length of the car, then got down on hands and knees to peer under the front end, back toward the steering wheel. The reaction from his stomach was spontaneous. Jumping to his feet, he reeled back, retching as he ran. The eagle cocked his head and shifted from one talon to another.

Hands shaking, Brian hit the walkie-talkie button on the

car phone. "I don't care if he's in a meeting," he said, "put me through! This is an emergency."

"Okay, okay, slow down, son," said Bob Miller, his supervisor. "Now start over. What did you say the condition is?"

"DRT," said Brian, inadvertently using their office acronym for a road kill of any kind: Dead Right There.

two

Heaven seems a little closer in a house beside the water.

—Anonymous

Arms crossed as he leaned back against the kitchen counter, Paul Osborne pondered the two pints of fresh-picked raspberries sitting on the table in front of him. He was considering making an angel food cake. Angel food topped with fresh raspberries. Can't beat that. And you have to share.

He liked that thought. Good reason to invite a certain woman to dinner. Well, maybe an hour or two in the trout stream first and then some dinner. Followed by—who knows? He could get lucky.

So far the northern Wisconsin weather was cooperating. Unseasonably cool temperatures paired with winds out of the northwest may have disappointed tourists that August, but they sure kept the fly-fishermen happy. Cool, windy weather meant fewer bugs, which meant hungry trout. Add fresh raspberries to that equation and Osborne had an excellent excuse for an invitation.

He reached for the beat-up three-ring binder in which his late wife, Mary Lee, had kept family recipes. The angel food cake recipe was from his Aunt Olive, his mother's sister. She had taken over the household after his mother's death. He was six that year—the year she lived with Osborne and his father. The following year, thank the Lord, his father sent him off to boarding school.

Angel food cake was the only pleasant memory he had of Aunt Ollie, a sharp-tongued, sharp-faced woman who seemed older than her years. Rail thin and tall, she had towered over him as she raged. In contrast, the Jesuit boarding school with its rules and regulations was a relief. At least you knew what was going to happen—and why.

Osborne scanned his aunt's faded script. Her list of ingredients looked simple enough. But did he have the utensils? He could still see her beating the egg whites in the big old ceramic mixing bowl. She beat them by hand. She beat him by hand, too.

A pan. He needed the right pan. Osborne wheeled around in his chair, then knelt to dig through one of the lower cupboards. He was sure there was an angel food cake pan in there somewhere. Ah! Reaching way to the back, he found it.

He stood up. Egg whites—he would need a special whisk. Certainly he could use the electric mixer, but he wanted to do this the old-fashioned way. How well he remembered the magic of those egg whites billowing up. And Aunt Ollie had insisted on a certain kind of whisk for angel food. He thought Mary Lee had used one just like it.

Searching through the utensil drawer, it dawned on him that Aunt Ollie and his late wife had more in common than just a whisk. Was that why he'd married Mary Lee? Because the coldness and criticism felt familiar? He shook his head. At least he didn't have that to worry about anymore.

He found a whisk, but it was rusted. Ray might have one. If his neighbor could keep an antique phone booth in the living room of his mobile home, why not an old whisk in his kitchen drawer?

Glancing out the window, he was reminded that the day was sunny and warm—just right for a walk. Since it was early afternoon, chances were good Ray would be home. A fishing guide, he tended to book clients in the early morning and after dusk. Of course, if he'd been called to dig a grave or two that day, he might be out.

What the heck—Osborne decided to amble on down to Ray's. Mike needed the exercise and the black Lab loved racing through the woods with Ray's yellow Labs, Ruff and Ready, whose antics with Mike always put a grin on Osborne's face.

Just as he opened the screen door to let the dog out into the yard, the phone rang.

"Doc?" The lean, quiet voice lifted his heart.

"Lew—you caught me just in time. I was about to walk out the door—"

"Anything you can cancel?" she said, interrupting him. "I need help and I need it now."

"Sure, what's up?" Osborne said, walking back into the kitchen and reaching for a notepad. He'd been half-expecting a call. Half-hoping was more like it.

Just that morning over coffee with his buddies at McDonald's, they had been grousing about the Loon Lake Country Music Fest. Every third week of August it happened: total gridlock. Main Street, restaurants, bars, even the Loon Lake Market overflowed with people wearing too much suntan lotion, too little clothing, and reeking of alcohol.

For nearly a decade, twenty-two thousand country music fans had been descending on Loon Lake, Pop. 3,412—cramming trailers, RVs, pickups, and cars into the campgrounds and motels surrounding the little town. For six days the wail and thump of country music would echo across the water. Great for the local economy, but it made for one long week for Loon Lake's law enforcement team.

Even with reinforcements from the sheriff, the exuberance generated by the music and the round-the-clock consumption of beer, beer, and more beer would overwhelm Chief Lewellyn Ferris and her three-man Loon Lake Police Department. From fender benders to fist fights, the list of alcohol-fueled incidents left no room for anything more than routine police work.

"Nothing serious, I hope," said Osborne.

"Oh-h-h, it's serious. The Forest Service called in to report a car accident. Fatality. One of the rangers found it back on that abandoned road north of County A. You know where I mean?"

"Oh, yeah. I've been back in there bird hunting. But, Lew, no one drives that road—it dead-ends."

"Likely a drunk who took a wrong turn. And, darn it anyway, it's right on the township border. One-half a mile to the north and I could off-load it onto Vilas County. As it is, someone has to check it out, but I cannot possibly get away from here for another hour. I've got a yahoo from Crandon who just caught his wife in the back of his pickup with his best friend. Took off to get his gun."

"Lewellyn . . ." said Osborne, his voice tightening with worry.

"It's okay, I called over there and a Forest County deputy is already at the house. They'll put him in the hoosegow 'til he calms down. But I'm stuck with the guilty parties on this end until we know he's under control. So I hope you don't mind—"

"Just tell me what you need. An ID on the victim? Want me to get in touch with the family if the victim is a local?"

As he spoke, Osborne headed toward the den, where he kept his instrument bag. Since meeting Lew Ferris one night in a trout stream, he had been forever grateful for his stint in the military when he had been schooled in forensic dentistry. The better he had gotten to know her, the more he had made it a practice to keep current with new developments in the field. He might be retired from a full-time dental practice, but not from affairs of the heart.

Fortunately for Osborne, the Wausau Crime Lab was a distant seventy miles away and lacked the funding for a full-time odontologist. This put Lew in a position to deputize him whenever she needed an ID based on dental records.

On a few cases over the last two years, he had been able to help with background checks as well. Thirty-some years practicing dentistry in Loon Lake had taught him more about people than you could read in a dental chart. And he came cheap—whatever the budget, he was happy.

When the money wasn't there, he would bargain for another lesson in the trout stream. Lew was an expert fly-fisherman who'd been his first instructor. And last, if he could help it. While he knew his technique frustrated her—"Doc, you're losing way too many good trout flies!"—he was improving. Slowly. Slowly on purpose.

On water with a spinning rod, he was a seasoned fisherman with 51-inch muskie mounted over his fireplace to prove it. But the minute he pulled on waders, picked up a fly rod, stepped into a stiff current, and tried to cast a lure with the weight of a feather—the world changed. He was a rank beginner. And that had its advantages.

"If you could get to the site within the hour, that would be much appreciated. Oh, and one more favor?"

"Sure. But on one condition—" Before he could extend his invitation, she interrupted.

"I can't reach Pecore. Now why the hell would a coroner turn his phone off during the busiest week of the summer? Marlene called his neighbors and they told her he took his wife and mother-in-law out on the pontoon boat so they could listen to the music free from the water. Honestly, Doc, what a commode.

"So could you swing by the public landing and see if his car's there? If it is, leave a note on the windshield to meet you at the scene of the accident ASAP or I'll have his pension. And mark down the time you leave it, too. Guy needs to be a hell of a lot more accountable."

"Got it. Say, Lew, later this evening—"

"Uh-oh, here comes trouble. Later, Doc." She hung up before he could say another word.

Darn, thought Osborne as he placed the cordless phone back in its stand. He called in a disappointed Mike and refilled the water bowl. Oh well, might get back too late to bake that cake anyway.

As he set the berries in the fridge, he plucked one from the top. Its rose red perfection prompted a vision of Lew's breasts in the moonlight. He entertained that thought. It was the kind of daydream that in his youth had led the Jesuit confessor to levy a penance of six Hail Marys and six Our Fathers: a venial sin well worth the prayers.

He would have to stop by Ray's to borrow a whisk another time. Jumping into his Subaru, Osborne checked the gas to be sure he had enough to make it out to County A and the old highway.

Bob Miller missed the turnoff and had to double back. He was almost a mile down the road before he spotted Brian leaning back against the hood of his truck. The look on his face accused Miller of forgetting to include "discovery of corpses" in his job description.

"I called the police," said Miller as he walked over to put a reassuring arm across the shoulder of the white-faced young forester. "And your wife. I explained it would be a while until you got home. Shouldn't take too long to remove the body."

"The *body*?" said Brian. "Bob, there are three women in that car."

three

Fish now. You're dead for a long time.

—Anonymous

The eagle persisted—not even the arrival of more vehicles could dissuade him. Osborne was the third to arrive, not long after Bob Miller. Five minutes at the public landing was all he had needed to locate Pecore's boat of a Town Car in the sea of SUVs and wedge a scrap of paper under the windshield wiper.

The note included a handwritten map a kindergartner could follow along with Lew's request that Pecore get to the scene of the accident "ASAP." Osborne jotted his initials along with the time—not that he expected that to make a difference. The throb and whine of Country Fest drifting across the water made it highly unlikely Pecore would be back soon.

Cresting a hill on the old highway, Osborne spotted the two men and their trucks parked across from the overturned car. A baby blue convertible. He knew that car. Only one person in Loon Lake drove a car that color: custom painted to match her fingernails. The sunny August day turned dark and shot through with dread.

Osborne slowed to pull in behind the Forest Service vehicles. He recognized Bob Miller. He sat three pews behind him at eight o'clock Mass every Sunday. The young man with him must be on his staff.

"That's Peg Garmin's car," said Osborne, loping past the two foresters toward the wreck, hoping against hope that the report of a fatality was wrong. "Chief Ferris sent me out to help with the recovery and identification of the victim."

"Well, Doc, you got more than one trapped in there—three women far as I can tell," said Miller. "Got an eagle in that tree over your head's done some damage, too."

"No sign of life?"

"No-o-o sirree. Brian here came across the vehicle on his way home about an hour ago. That right, Brian—an hour would you say?" Brian nodded from where he was leaning against his truck, arms folded. The young man looked queasy and not a little frightened, as if he was worried he might be asked to approach the car again.

Kneeling to peer under the car, Osborne thrust his head forward, then backed off fast. "Whoa!" He paused, then bent forward again. This time with caution.

The car had rolled with its top down. The bodies of two women were compressed at strange angles in the front seat; a third had been thrown half out of the rear seat. Her torso rested on the ground with her head twisted back as if searching for something behind her. Too bad she had been injured, thought Osborne. He could see plenty of room for that victim to have crawled out.

In spite of the damage done by the eagle, he had no doubt the driver was Peg Garmin. The cloud of pale blond hair was dark with dried blood; those snappy blue eyes would never laugh again. Osborne reached through the twisted steering wheel, his fingers gentle on her eyelids: Someone had to say good-bye. No matter how harsh the gossip he had heard from his late wife and her friends, he had always liked Peg Garmin.

For all the darkness in her life, she had been a woman of light and laughter, a woman with style: her hair done, her makeup fresh. That her loveliness had been for sale did not diminish it. How sad she would be if she could see how she looked now. It crossed Osborne's mind to wonder if the eagle could have done *all* that damage. But, of course—had to be.

He stood up. "They've been here longer than an hour, that's for sure."

"Yep," said Bob. The three men stood in silence, nodding.

"Well, this sure is more than Chief Ferris was planning on," said Osborne. "Bob, you got a cell phone or a radio in that truck of yours? I need to let Marlene on the switchboard know that I'll need at least one more ambulance to get these poor folks to the morgue."

"Sure, Doc, you're welcome to use our radio. Here, I'll set you up."

As Osborne reached for the walkie-talkie, a distant rumbling could be heard heading their way. "That may be the EMTs now," said Osborne.

But it was a tow truck that crested the rise.

four

The great fish eat the small.

—Alexander Barclay

With Osborne and Bob standing by to let him know when to stop, Robbie Mikkleson swung his tow truck around, then backed it in tight to the rear end of the overturned convertible. He was the police department's favored tow operator: fair in his pricing and gentle with his touch. Even insurance adjusters loved him.

The burly thirty-year-old was also a close friend of Osborne's neighbor, at whose home he could be found, on random weekdays, savoring a midmorning cup of coffee doused with local gossip and a round-up of who-caught-what-where. In return, he managed to keep Ray's rusty red pickup running against all odds. While he couldn't unlock the frozen passenger side door or replace its broken window, he was able to keep fuel flowing.

Robbie wasn't bad on small engines either, and had repaired Osborne's Mercury 9.9 outboard after the prop took a clobbering from an unmarked, submerged boulder. And like Ray, he knew just about everyone in Loon Lake: If you were over sixteen and driving a vehicle in the land of ice and snow, sooner or later you met Robbie. The motto painted across the hood of his truck was designed to salve wounded wallets: DITCHES HAPPEN.

"Hey there," said the big guy, dropping down from the seat of his truck with a thud. "Heard on the scanner you need a tow out here."

Robbie's broad, friendly face floated above a summer uniform that never changed: denim overalls hooked over a greasy sweatshirt that may have been white once upon a time and whose stretched-out cuffs were rolled up over his elbows. He sported a four-day stubble on his cheeks and a band of sweat across his forehead. As he walked toward Osborne, he was grinning the grin of a man tickled to earn an unexpected eighty-five bucks—until he got a good look at the overturned car. He whistled then said, "Doggone, *baby blue*? That has to be Peg Garmin's car. Don't tell me *she's* in there?"

"Afraid so," said Osborne. "Couple other victims as well. Haven't been able to get a good look at those two yet. Maybe you can help me move things around a little so I can."

"Sure thing, Doc . . . doggone . . ." Robbie repeated himself as he walked around the wreck. He knelt on the far side, near the passenger seat and across from where Osborne stood. "Oh . . . that's too bad," he said. "I know those ladies. Played a few hands of poker with Donna just last week."

He got to his feet, eyes searching every exposed surface. Eyes as expert as Osborne's when examining the mouth of a new patient. "Boy oh boy," he said after a long minute of deliberation, "I can't figure this out. Just how the hell did they manage to do this?"

"Donna who?" said Osborne. "What's her last name? Any idea who that gal in the back might be?"

"Donna's last name is Federer," said Robbie, "You

might know her old man. He used to drive for Johnson Septic—Ralph Federer."

"Oh, sure," said Osborne. He remembered Ralph. He remembered Ralph's cheap, awful dentures better.

"I can see better after we raise the vehicle," said Robbie, "but that woman in the backseat looks a lot like Pat Kuzynski to me—same hair anyway. Those two—Donna and Pat—both been working at Thunder Bay, y'know."

"Oh," said Osborne. Knowing Peg, that didn't surprise him. "Strippers, I take it."

"Yep. Jeez, doggone. I liked those gals. Always friendly."

"Too bad they didn't befriend a designated driver," said Osborne.

"Boy, I dunno," said Robbie, scratching his head. "I seen people walk away from rollovers worse than this. Especially drunks—they never get hurt. Thrown out, doncha know—but not hurt. Hell, the gas tank didn't even explode on this one."

As Osborne watched, Robbie continued to examine the exposed underbelly of the car, then walked around to unscrew the gas cap. As he did so, Bob Miller and Brian backed away so fast they bumped into each other, stumbled, and nearly fell.

"No worry," said Robbie. "Looks safe enough even though that tank sure is topped off. Man, if this tank had blown—we'd have heard it in town." He pulled a kerchief from his back pocket and wiped his face. "Jeez, it's hot. You sure as hell don't want these folks sitting here much longer—whaddya say I hook her up and get things rolling?"

"Hold off a few more minutes, Robbie," said Osborne. "Chief Ferris needs the coroner to take a few photos—a case with fatalities, you never know. Could be litigation by

the families, questions from the insurance agency—we
have to wait."

"Not a problem," said Robbie. "Who we waiting on?
Ol' Dog Face Pecore?"

"Unfortunately."

"Wouldn't you think they could rid of that joker?"

"Political appointee," said Osborne, shaking his head.

Few people in Loon Lake accorded their coroner much respect. Before Lewellyn Ferris took over as Chief of the
Loon Lake Police Department, Irv Pecore had run his own
shop—partly because he wasn't needed very often, partly
because dealing with the dead had been one chore Lew's
predecessors had been happy to assign to someone else.

For twenty years, he had conducted autopsies on his
own schedule and often under less than sanitary circumstances—the worst of which was allowing both his golden
retrievers to observe the procedures. Every one in Loon
Lake knew it, and more than one set of anxious relatives
had accompanied their dearly departed through the un-
comfortable process just to be sure canine interest was
halted at the door.

But while Pecore's position was secure due to the fact
his brother-in-law was the mayor, Lew had been able to
cite enough violations of the chain of custody on evidence
that she was able to gain control over a significant portion
of his budget.

That made it possible for her to limit his involvement in
criminal investigations and allot the monies to bring in the
Wausau Crime Lab or professionals like Osborne. With her
appointment to Chief of the Loon Lake Police Department,
the dogs were banned, the evidence storage improved, and
Pecore put on notice that he was likely to be terminated
with the next mayoral election: no kin, no job.

• • •

"If I hoist this about four feet," said Robbie, pointing to the back end of the car, "you should be able to remove the victims. Won't take long after that."

"Oh boy," said Osborne, checking his watch for the tenth time, "I hate this waiting. Hold on a minute." He walked over to where Brian and Bob were standing. "Bob, you wouldn't happen to have a camera in your car, would you?"

"Sorry, Doc."

"Mind if I use that radio of yours again?" The forester gave him a nod.

"Marlene," said Osborne, "it's me again. Robbie's here with the tow truck and still no sign of Pecore or an ambulance. We really need to get a move on getting these victims out of the wreck. Could you check with Chief Ferris and see what she thinks about getting Ray out here with his camera? This time of day he's usually home.

"Oh—and let her know one of the deceased, the driver, is Peg Garmin. Robbie's pretty sure of the other two victims, too," said Osborne. "Donna Federer and Pat Kuzynski, but that's not official yet. Thank you, Marlene."

"Dr. Osborne," said Brian, as Osborne got out of Bob's vehicle, "how long do you need me to stay?"

"Poor guy's trying to leave on his vacation," said Bob.

His back to the wreck, Osborne looked over at the two men. "This is going to take a while. I see no need for either of you to hang around. Brian, since you were the first on the scene of the accident, can you give me a phone number in case Chief Ferris has any questions?"

As he spoke, he heard a grinding from the tow truck and turned to see the convertible shifting upward. "No!" shouted Osborne. "Not yet!"

"Just testing," hollered Robbie from his cab. It was obvious he couldn't hear Osborne over the sound of the winch. Osborne watched helpless as the car was lifted far enough off the ground that the two women in the front seat, strapped in with seat belts, now looked like riders on a macabre roller coaster. The body of the third woman rolled onto the ground. She lay on her back, face up.

"Oh, jeez," said Bob. Brian turned away. Osborne hurried over to kneel near the body. He tipped the head to one side.

"Oh my God," he said, his voice soft. He didn't need dental forensics to tell him he was looking at the effects of a bullet fired at close range, a bullet that entered the left temple.

"Sorry, Doc, I wasn't thinking," said Robbie, rushing up from behind. Osborne motioned for him to stay back. He checked the two bodies in the front seat.

Three women, three bullets, three victims all right. No accident.

five

*You can't say enough about fishing. Though the sport of
kings, it's just what the deadbeat ordered.*

—Thomas McGuane, *Silent Seasons*

"**He-e-y,** you Jack Pine savage," said Robbie, his voice
booming as he sauntered over to where Ray had just
jammed his pickup into reverse. Following a wave of Robbie's hand, Ray backed up to park twenty feet from the
front of the tow truck.

He had arrived just as Brian and Bob were leaving,
making it necessary for Robbie to direct him to the opposite side of the road. The cloud of dust thrown up by the
departing Forest Service trucks coupled with his own tires'
skidding in reverse made it difficult to see beyond the tow
truck. With the help of the tag alder along the side of the
road, the overturned vehicle was completely obscured.

As the pickup came to a stop, Robbie walked over. He
leaned into the open window. "What the hell was that I
heard on the police scanner this morning?" he said, thrusting his face at Ray. "You assaulted some poor woman with
a dead fish?"

"I . . . did not . . . *assault* . . . anyone," said Ray, of-
fended. "It was a ri-*dic*-u-lous sit-u-a-tion. . . . B-i-i-g . . .
mis . . . understanding." His habit of mixing pauses with

elongated syllables had been known to drive more than one listener away. But Robbie was wise to his tricks. He wasn't going anywhere until he got the whole story.

"All right, all right," said Ray, raising a hand in defeat. "All that happened was I was down at the post office minding my own business and some goofy state cop tried to put me in the hoosegow for smelling walleyes with one of the nuns I know. And that's the whole story."

As the clouds of dust settled, he caught sight of Osborne coming around from the front of the tow truck. He craned his neck past Robbie to shout: "Hey, Doc! I phoned Channel Twelve and told 'em to send a news crew out here."

"Jeez, Ray. Why the hell did you do *that*?" said Osborne, not a little annoyed. The last thing Lew Ferris needed right now was a TV crew tramping over evidence. He kicked at a chunk of gravel on the road, then planted his feet, crossed his arms, and glared at Ray still sitting in the cab of the battered red pickup.

"For what it's worth, I suggest you get the photos taken care of *now*. The sun is good and high and we've got a shot at some definition if we find any tracks near the crash site—before your TV people mess it up."

He knew he was wasting energy. Three years of living next door to the guy coupled with three years of fishing in the same boat had taught Paul Osborne the reality of life with Ray. He could be guaranteed to move with speed on only two occasions: one was to set a hook, the other to save a life.

Otherwise, as every member of the morning McDonald's coffee crowd would swear, based on personal experience, you were held hostage to "Ray time": The more he was needed, the slower he was likely to move.

Proving the point, Ray unfolded his six feet five inches

from the cramped interior of the pickup section by section. Watching him reminded Osborne of the aluminum wading staff Lew had given him for his birthday: its nine-inch links, separated and folded in on themselves, needed only a shake to lengthen and lock in.

Ray paused to adjust his belt and pluck at the folds of his shirt. That's when it dawned on Osborne. No wonder it had taken the guy forty-five minutes to get there: That razzbonya was dressed for a photo op!

In a challenge to the heat and humidity of the afternoon, he was decked out in pressed khakis, an equally well-ironed khaki fishing shirt (sleeves rolled with care to just above the elbows), and a deerskin vest, fringed below the shoulders. A sterling silver walleye, pinned above the fringe on the left shoulder, glinted in the sunlight.

Ray's auburn curls glistened, fresh from a shampoo and tousled with care to hang rakishly over his forehead. Even his beard, the auburn flecked with gray, had been tamed. Add to that a deep summer tan and dark eyes that sparkled with anticipation, and you had a fishing guide the ladies would love. Osborne groaned: Only Ray could turn a homicide into an audition.

"Hey, you haven't answered me yet—what do you mean, *smelling walleyes*?" said Robbie, his voice insistent as he stepped back to let Ray pass. Ray frowned. Osborne was curious himself by now. Robbie was on to something—maybe Ray *had* spent the morning in jail.

"Marlene said you got a triple murder out here—that's *big*," said Ray, determined to change the subject. "Could make *network* news—network *evening* news—you never know."

Osborne shook his head. The guy was a hound for attention when it came to the media.

Ray was convinced that talent scouts would someday

realize he was a natural to replace David Letterman: "Think about it, Doc," he would say, twisting a lock of his beard as he ruminated over a grilled cheese sandwich in Osborne's kitchen. "What does ol' Dave have that I don't? I'm good-looking, I'm different, and *I'm* funny."

Not that he wasn't willing to compromise: host of the Outdoors Channel would work. In the meantime, aware that a number of television professionals out of Chicago vacationed in the northwoods, Ray never missed an opportunity to—as he put it—"catch air time."

Yep, Ray never lost hope that some lucky day a producer would drive up to that lurid muskie-green house trailer of his, barge through the doorway outlined with the raked teeth of the ferocious "shark of the north," and slam a multiyear contract down on his kitchen table.

Until that happened, he trained for fame by inflicting his humor on clients. Some got a kick out of the bad jokes, caught big fish, tipped well, and came back for more. Others winced, caught big fish, tipped modestly, and were never seen again. But Ray had faith in his credentials, and Osborne, along with his McDonald's buddies, agreed: Ray was indeed *different*.

Given that the economics of life as a fishing guide were as chancy as the weather in the northwoods, he shored up his fluctuating income by digging graves in the summer, plowing snow in the winter, and selling a few photos— more and more each season. The latter not by accident as the photography mirrored Ray's passions.

He might be a man of modest means but he lived a life rich with the outdoors: days packed with opportunities to capture eagles, foxes, loons, otters—even wolves—in the lens of the camera he carried in his tackle box. Each autumn a few of those photos would find their way to a local printer, who paid him ten bucks each for use on the calendars given away by local insurance agencies.

His sister, a wealthy trial lawyer in Chicago, had tried to convince him that he had such a good eye, he might make it as a professional photographer. But that sounded too much like a day job to Ray. Only when Chief Lewellyn Ferris needed him would Ray—as he put it—"go pro." The work for the Loon Lake Police Department was short term, paid well, and rarely interfered with his fishing.

And if he was happy, Lew was more so. Deputizing Ray to photograph a crime scene allowed her to circumvent Pecore's sloppiness—with minimal damage to the department budget. Better yet, it allowed her to tap into Ray's talent for tracking.

His instinct for light and dark and all the shades between made him an expert tracker. That, plus the hours he'd spent on water and in the woods since he was a kid. Unlike the boys from the Wausau Crime Lab, who worked best indoors (when she was able to twist their arms to drive sixty-seven miles north), Ray excelled in the forests, along the shorelines, down country roads and logging lanes. That's where he could see what was missing, what was disturbed, what lay beyond the obvious.

But it was never easy to persuade him to take the job. He was too accustomed to being on the receiving end of law enforcement. "Hey," he would argue, "if I keep this up, my buddies'll think I'm undercover—no one'll fish with me."

"I need you, Ray," Lew would counter, "you think like a criminal. Who else can fish private water and never get caught?"

"Okay, okay, here's what happened and it's *not* what you heard on the police scanner," said Ray, convinced at last that Robbie had no intention of letting him off the hook.

"I was minding my own business and driving by the post office when I saw Sister Rita. As Doc here knows, every Friday I drop a string of bluegills and a couple walleyes off at the convent. The nuns love 'em. And every Friday I try to explain how good those fish smell right after they're caught. Which is true—right?"

"Right," said Robbie. Osborne nodded. That is true of fresh-caught walleye.

"So happens this morning I had a couple walleyes that I'd just caught when I see Sister Rita in the parking lot of the post office. Right away I pull over, drop the gate on my truck, and just as I'm holding up a twenty-inch beauty for Sister Rita to smell, the damn state cop drives up—"

"I don't suppose you were wearing that stuffed trout on your head, were ya?" said Robbie, interrupting.

"Yes, I was—but what would that have to do with any-thing?" said Ray, sounding hurt.

"Well—the cop mighta thought you were full of baloney."

"You'd think he'd believe a nun! Sister Rita tried to tell him all we were doing was smelling fish."

"Ray—don't ever change, man," said Robbie, wide shoulders heaving as he chuckled. "I gotta tell 'ya, listen-ing to the scanner this morning made my day. Sure did. Oh, jeez." He wiped a tear from his eye.

"More fun for you than for me," said Ray.

"Ray—got the camera?" said Osborne. Enough time had been wasted.

"Yep, right here." He reached through the open window for his camera and the hat in question. "I was embarrassed, Sister Rita was embarrassed. The guy just didn't get it. *And* he made an unkind remark about my hat."

Holding it with both hands as if afraid it might break, Ray set the stuffed trout on his head, then bent to check the angle in the truck's side mirror. He tipped the fish slightly to the right then stooped to lean in for a closer look.

"Drats . . ." He lifted it off, huffed on the silver lure that was draped across the trout's neck, and with a gentle touch, rubbed the lure on his sleeve until it shone. Again he set the hat on his head, giving it a tip to the right. He winked at Robbie: "Just in case *that* story hits the networks."

"Ray, I really wish you hadn't notified the TV station," said Osborne, beckoning for Ray to follow him down the road past the tow truck. "Lew put a call in to the Wausau boys but I have no idea when they'll get here. We can't have anyone getting close to the victims and the wreck until they're finished."

"I hear ya, Doc, and I'll make sure that doesn't happen." Ray slung the camera strap around his neck.

"You and I have to be careful, too. You'll see an entry path that I set up so we disturb as little of the site as possible."

"Okedoke." Ray ambled along behind Osborne. It wasn't until they had cleared the front of the tow truck that Ray got a good view of the suspended convertible and its occupants.

"Wha—!" He gave a strangled bark of pain and disbelief—then yanked the camera from his neck and thrust it at Osborne. He dashed for the car. Two feet from the front of the wreck, he fell to his hands and knees and froze, eyes fixed on the body dangling from the driver's seat.

Osborne heard him gasp. "What? That's a bullet wound!"

"Yes," said Osborne. He stopped a few feet back from Ray. "Three women were riding in that car. All three . . . executed."

Ray's eyes raked the scene in front of him. At last he stood, his body stiff, his back to Osborne. "Why didn't you tell me it was Peg?"

Osborne threw his arms up. This was too much. For nearly two hours he and Robbie had been waiting—unable to do anything about a sad and gruesome reality until photos were shot and the team from the crime lab arrived—and now he was accused of doing something wrong?

"Ray, I had no idea you know the woman well enough that it would matter."

Ray mumbled something.

"What? I didn't hear you . . ."

Only then did Osborne realize he was weeping.

"I said, 'She was my mother's closest friend.'" Ray stood up and turned around, eyes dull with grief.

"How . . . what . . ." Osborne didn't know where to begin.

"They were friends for years . . . she was the first woman I ever loved."

Osborne was stunned. The Peg Garmin he knew was soft-spoken, gracious, and lovely in a pale, ethereal way—remarkable for a woman in her line of work. But the fact remained, she was a call girl. An expensive call girl. *And* a close friend of the wife of the town's most prominent physician? Ray's first love? Something didn't fit.

He was silent as Ray walked toward him, reaching for the camera.

"I'll take care of this," said Ray. And Osborne knew he was talking about a lot more than just the photos.

six

I want fish from fishing, but I want a great deal more than that, and getting it is not always dependent on catching fish.

Roderick Haig-Brown

It was ninety-two in the shade and the cicadas were screaming when Lew's cruiser finally cleared the hill. The team from the Wausau Crime Lab beat her by thirty minutes and had already roped off the area around the wreck. Right behind the police cruiser, fueling a block-long cloud of dust, came two ambulances.

"Doc—" Lew slammed the car door behind her and shouted to Osborne, who, along with Robbie, was leaning against the his car, "Do you mind asking the EMTs to stay back until I can talk to the Wausau boys? Sorry to keep you waiting—be with you in a second."

"I'll take care of it," said Osborne. "Lew, don't rush. A few more minutes won't make a difference." Not to him at least. And the EMTs were likely to appreciate the fact that the delay plus the heat was loosening the hold of rigor mortis on the victims, which would make their jobs a little easier.

"Don't worry about me," said Robbie. With no calls for tows and the hours on this job adding up, he was happy.

"The longer it takes, the richer I get," he had confided in Osborne.

With the long reporter-style notebook that she favored in hand, Lew circled the wreck. She would take a few steps, stop to jot a few notes, then continue. Osborne watched from where he stood. As always, he found her easy on the eyes—particularly today as the heat had forced her to undo the top three buttons of her shirt.

Osborne was always surprised by how strongly he was attracted to this woman who was the opposite of his late wife. Where Mary Lee would never think of leaving the house without a full-scale application of makeup and every strand of hair anchored with spray, Lew could care less. He doubted she owned any makeup, certainly no hairspray. The few times he had spent the night at her farmhouse, the closest thing to makeup that he could find in her medicine cabinet was sunscreen.

And where Mary Lee had been small-boned and bragged of being allergic to any exercise beyond a short walk—Lew Ferris wouldn't hesitate to load herself down with a fully inflated float tube, a fly-fishing vest with every pocket filled, a fly rod, and a backpack stuffed with waders, wading boots, sandwiches, fruit, nuts, and two bottles of water. That was *before* hiking in two miles to a secret lake for an afternoon of playing with brook trout.

Nor was Lew Ferris a small woman but sturdy, trim, and strong and with a curve to her hips that was emphasized by the crisp tan pants that constituted half the summer uniform of the department. The uniform's other half was a matching cotton shirt that, even unbuttoned, fit snugly across her breasts. Osborne knew better than to tell her how good she looked in that uniform. God forbid she decide to wear a larger shirt!

Lew edged her way around the overturned convertible and stooped twice to get a closer look at the victims. Walking back toward Osborne, she paused to converse in low tones with the two forensic specialists who'd driven up from Wausau. While she spoke, Osborne searched her face for signs of fatigue. The Country Fest crowd partied around the clock, which meant that even with help from neighboring police departments, Lew had been working sixteen-hour days. But if she was tired, it didn't show. At least not to his eyes.

What he saw was a frank, open face tanned dark by the summer sun. Her cheeks were flushed from the heat, her dark eyes serious and calculating. Dark brown curls tumbled across her forehead and over her ears as if uncaged by the humid air. As she spoke to the two men, she raised one arm to wipe away the perspiration gleaming on her forehead.

"Whoa—this heat is something," said Lew. "How soon before we can move these bodies?"

"Give us a little more time," said the taller of the two men. "We need to bag the hands of each of the victims and protect those door handles before letting anyone approach."

Osborne recognized Bruce Peters, who had managed a Wausau forensic team on a murder case for the Loon Lake Police the previous winter. A tall man in his early thirties, Bruce had friendly brown eyes and a large, square head that reminded Osborne of Mike, his black Lab.

He was also an aspiring fly-fisherman who had been badgering Lew to help him with his casting. So far no date had worked for both parties and Osborne hoped it never would—or that he could maneuver to invite himself along. Bruce didn't wear a wedding ring, and who knew how he felt about dating older women. Vigilance was merited.

Lew motioned to Robbie to walk over to where she was standing. "Bruce, this is Rob Mikkleson. When you and your partner are ready, he'll be towing the vehicle down to Wausau," she said.

"Chief Ferris—something you might want to consider," said Robbie. "I've got a clean, open area—pretty well lit—in one of my garages. These fellas are welcome to work on the vehicle there. Might save the cost of towing it all the way to Wausau."

"He's got a point," said Bruce. "Hauling it sixty miles on the interstate might dislodge any trace evidence that could be critical."

"That's fine with me," said Lew.

"How 'bout the black box—will you guys be checking that?" said Robbie.

Bruce gave the tow operator a puzzled look.

"Late-model cars like this Chrysler have data recorders that record how the air bags work. Some can tell you if the cruise control, traction control, and the stability control were on. Might be worth checking—a buddy of mine who's a mechanic for the Chrysler dealer over in Rhinelander has a diagnostic computer that'll run that analysis if you want."

"What good would that do?" said Bruce, sounding peeved that a burly guy in a dirty sweatshirt and overalls might one-up their forensic results.

"Can't say exactly," said Robbie, "but if I were you, I'd sure like to know what happened during those last five seconds before this vehicle rolled. You want my two cents, I find the setup here"—he waved an arm at the wreck—"to be damn peculiar. And I seen a lotta wrecks . . ."

"Peculiar?" said Lew.

"Yeah," said Robbie. "Peculiar." Everyone stared at the overturned convertible with its grim cargo for a long moment.

"Can't say I've ever seen anything like it before myself—won't hurt to check it out," said Lew.

"Robbie, you said something earlier that I think you should mention to Chief Ferris," said Osborne. "About the gas tank."

"Oh, yeah, almost forgot," said Robbie. "I told Doc here that tank is so full, I can't believe it didn't explode."

"Topped off?" said Lew.

"Pretty close," said Robbie. "They had to have filled that tank within the last thirty, forty miles I'd say."

"Well, that narrows our search to a forty-mile radius," said Lew. "Little overwhelming with everything else going on in Loon Lake. Doc"—she turned to Osborne—"I'm hoping you and Ray can help out for the next day or two. Ray can't be doing much fishing in this weather—"

"I don't have a problem with that," said Osborne. He resisted the impulse to hold up his right hand for a congratulatory slap—just the way twelve-year-old Beth, his granddaughter, celebrated every smallmouth she caught off the end of his dock.

Instead, he managed a mock grimace so the Wausau boys wouldn't catch on to how pleased he was to be drafted as a deputy again. He had to be the only retired dentist who loved returning to work—work that might generate modest pay but offered the unique benefit of a boss he never tired of seeing. Crime may not pay for some folks, but it had a way of making Osborne's day.

Robbie glanced at his watch then over at Bruce, "How long you think before I can move this?"

"Well . . ." Bruce gave Lew an inquiring look. "When's showtime?" He winked and grinned like a little kid.

"Hah!" snorted Lew. "No wonder you made such good time getting up here. No one pulled you over for speeding, I hope."

"Nah, we just hightailed it the minute after you called."

Lew gave a low chuckle. "So *that's* the secret to getting you Wausau boys on the scene when I need you."

"Yep. Got the tickets?"

"As promised." Lew unbuttoned the shirt pocket over her left breast.

"What time does she go on?"

"They told me ten o'clock at the earliest."

"Plenty of time for us to get all the preliminaries under way here."

"What's that all about?" asked Osborne as he and Lew headed over to where the EMTs were waiting.

"Country Fest has been making up for all the extra hours we've had work with free tickets to the shows," said Lew. "When I called down to Wausau and said I had tickets to see Shania Twain tonight—I had *instant* cooperation."

A smile of satisfaction crossed her face and Osborne knew why. This was a marked improvement in her usual relations with "those goddam Wausau boys." The lead supervisor of the Wausau Crime Lab was not one of Lew's favorite people—nor she his. Close to retirement age, Chuck Meyer was a former FBI agent who had little respect for women in the military or in law enforcement.

Whenever she needed assistance from his lab—assistance for which Loon Lake had to pay good money—he found ways to make it clear that he considered Police Chief Lewellyn Ferris to be way out of her league.

It was always the same battle: He would respond to her request with a snide remark implying that a man in her position would be able to handle the situation, whatever it was. She would listen to his rant, and when he had finished, in a calm voice she would list the resources and manpower needed. She would then request that he fax her a proposed budget and timeline. Chuck would balk, insisting he needed at least twenty-four hours advance notice.

"Fine," Lew would say, "I'll send down a few figures." Which she would do within thirty minutes—but only after trimming the projected costs by thirty percent. This would send Chuck into a frenzy. Within fifteen minutes, he would fire back an adjusted budget, which Lew would walk over to the home of the Loon Lake mayor for approval. The routine was repeated every couple of months—and Chuck never caught on.

Today, when Lew called in, he was on vacation and Bruce was in charge. Bruce, who was bored, a Shania Twain fan, and, Osborne suspected, pleased to be working again with Lew. She found him willing to negotiate without paperwork and—once the free tickets were mentioned—running for the parking lot.

"Where's Ray?" said Lew, looking around after instructing the EMTs. "He didn't leave, did he? I'll need more photos once they have those bodies ready for transport. Cost a bloody fortune if I have to have Bruce shoot 'em."

"He drove up the road about forty-five minutes ago," said Osborne. "I examined the victim who rolled out of the backseat and the pattern of postmortem lividity indicates she did not die sitting in the car. She died standing up—which may be true of all three. Ray wanted to backtrack the direction the car was traveling to see if he might find any sign of where they were shot."

"He's been gone long enough, he must have found

something," said Lew. "Let's hope anyway. Any idea when all this may have happened?"

"Not with this hot weather," said Osborne. "Afraid I have to defer to the pathologist on that."

Lew nodded. "I had Marlene call out to Thunder Bay and Robbie was right—neither Donna Federer nor Pat Kuzynski showed up for work last night. She reached Pat's mother, who was on the verge of calling us. Donna lives alone but Marlene put a call in to her father. I've arranged for them to meet us at the hospital to identify the bodies. But when it comes to Peg Garmin, I don't know who we'll call."

"Ray knows the family and—"

"Family? I didn't know she had family. After her husband died, I thought . . ."

"Let's ask Ray when he gets back here," said Osborne. "He was pretty shook up, so I didn't ask any questions. But his mother and Peg were close. Ray has known Peg Garmin since he was a kid."

Lew was astonished. "Are you serious? Dr. Pradt's wife was a close friend of Peg Garmin's?" As she was shaking her head in disbelief, the battered red pickup rattled into view.

seven

Better to return and make a net, than to go down to the stream and merely wish for fish.

—Ancient proverb

The pickup skidded to a stop in front of the Loon Lake Police cruiser. Ray slammed the gearshift into neutral and, leaping from the driver's seat, shouted over at Lew, "Got it! Found the place where they were shot! Mile and a half down the road. You can see where they were run off. Even the tread marks of the vehicle that pulled 'em over—"

Lew looked up from her note taking. "You sure it's the same cars?"

"There's more." Ray's expression was grim.

"I'll follow you," said Lew, flipping the notebook closed as she jogged toward the police cruiser. "Doc, everything's under control here—need you to help me out." She motioned for Osborne to ride along.

Tires spinning, she pulled onto the gravel road behind Ray's truck, staying close to avoid the dust. About ninety seconds down the road, the pickup swerved to the right and stopped so fast Lew had all she could do to keep from rear-ending it. "Jeez Louise," she said, rolling down the car window as Ray came running up.

"Get out here," said Ray. "Any further, we might mess up some of those tread marks. I want you to follow me up the hill there—we're gonna circle back and around so we don't disturb anything." Ray spoke fast, his voice low.

"You think anyone is hiding back in there?" said Lew.

He gave her a quizzical look. "No. Oh no."

"Then can we slow the hell down and speak in a normal tone of voice? I almost took out your truck two seconds ago."

"Sorry," said Ray, "I just—you're right, no need to rush . . ."

Lew reached through the window to lay a hand on his shoulder. "We're all of us working this the best we can. Now settle down, will you?"

"Sure," said Ray.

But before Osborne and Lew could close the car doors, he was gone. And while Ray could move through a wall of aspen and across boulder-strewn hummocks as smoothly as a trout in water, the best that Lew and Osborne could do was stumble forward hoping not to trip and fall. The hill that Ray took in two leaps, they crawled up—clutching at clumps of grass for support. Pausing at the top to catch their breath, they skidded sideways, feet fighting gravity until the only option was to sit down and slide.

"Last thing I need right now is a twisted ankle," said Lew, wiping at the sweat on her forehead as she got to her feet.

"Or a branch in the eye," said Osborne, wondering why he took the time to brush dirt from his pants before plunging ahead. Twice they lost sight of Ray, only to catch glimpses of khaki bobbing and weaving through slash and past dead stumps. Just when they thought they *had* lost

him, they came around a stand of balsam to find him waiting.

He pointed off to the right. "We're not looking for a
brain surgeon—whoever shot Peg and those other two
women was dumb enough to throw their purses in the
bushes over there."

"Dammit!" said Lew, hands on her hips. "I *knew* something didn't fit when I was checking out that wreck. Just
couldn't put my finger on it—but that's it: the purses. You
don't find three women and *no purses*. One of their bags,
at least, would have been thrown from the vehicle when it
rolled."

"Good work, Ray," she said, emphasizing every word.
"Assuming it was the killer who threw them, let's pray for
decent prints . . . and more dumb mistakes."

"Walk slowly now," said Ray, his hand up in warning as
they neared the edge of a clearing surrounded by balsam,
spruce, and Norway pine. "Stop right where you are . . .
okay, take a look . . ."

Pools of something bright and black caught the light of
the lengthening sun: blood, tissue, flies. The bare trunks of
three tall pines had served a purpose.

"This is where it happened, all right," said Lew.

"Yes," said Ray, his voice soft as a prayer, "three people died here . . . one was like a sister to me . . ."

Neither Doc nor Lew spoke. There was nothing to say.
And Ray was a changed man. Gone was the lighthearted,
affable fishing guide of two hours earlier. In his place was
a somber, tense figure. A man who looked older than his
years.

Osborne had seen this man before—the night of his initial
visit to the room behind the door with the coffeepot on the
window. It was the first of many nights that he would lis-

ten to Ray tell his story. Over time their friendship flourished and Osborne came to know a side of Ray that few people did: the side that was driven. The side that woke every day determined to substitute water, monofilament, a lure, and the repetitive motion of casting for a more dangerous liquid addiction. An addiction bequeathed by his mother.

"I was walking over here—following the blood trails and taking photos—when I found the purses," said Ray as he guided Lew and Osborne along the edges of the clearing. "The killer was standing near that fallen log when the bags were thrown, and the footprints I found at that spot indicate whoever it was wore boots. Boots that left well-defined impressions.

"You can see for yourself the shine on the ground right there," he said, pointing. "See where the sole and heel compress the earth? Oh yes, I got close-ups, " he said, answering the question he saw in Lew's eyes.

"Be nice if we knew what kind of boots," she said.

"Not a hiking boot, I can tell you that," said Ray. "Most likely a cowboy boot but with a heel that left a distinct pattern. Over here and heading *towards* the clearing from the direction of the road, you can see tracks of four different pairs of shoes: two with heels, one without plus those boots.

"Something else that you *can't* see from here are long, chute-like impressions, which are hidden under that bank of ferns over there—"

"Drag marks?" said Lew.

"Yes. At least one body was dragged back towards the road—but some of the footprints in that direction, which are identical to the ones by the fallen log, are so well defined that I think the person walking was carrying additional weight. The odd thing about the boot prints is that they aren't any larger than the others—the ones from the shoes the women were wearing."

"So . . . another woman maybe?" said Osborne.

Ray shrugged, "Could be. So what I see here are the tracks of four people walking towards the clearing—then a separate trail back to the road. That trail indicates weight being dragged or carried by only one person, a person whose footprints are identical to those around the fallen log. Now, I left prints myself when I first got here but I was very careful not to step any closer to those tracks than I had to for the photos—"

"You're wearing moccasins, Ray. Bruce will know your prints from the others easily," said Lew.

"Right. One more thing—whoever left those boot prints has been here before."

Lew gave Ray a long look. "Are you saying the shootings were premeditated?"

"Well, take a look over here and see what you think," said Ray, motioning for them to follow him twenty feet to the right of where they had been standing.

"Even though we haven't had rain for over a week, the forest canopy overhead protects the ground—allows it to hold moisture while the evergreens block the wind. I was able to find an older set of tracks leading back here, parallel to the paths taken by the three victims and the killer." Ray motioned for them to halt, then pointed.

"That trail. Even though I'm just eyeballing it, I'm positive those tracks were made by the same boots that—"

"Okay, I've seen enough," said Lew. "I better let those Wausau boys know they have to work this site ASAP. No rain in the forecast for tonight, I hope."

"Not that I've heard," said Osborne.

"Poor Bruce," said Lew with a sigh. "There goes Shania Twain. Even if they tarp the site around the wreck, I doubt they can get enough done here in time to make the show. Doc, let's head back up the road and deliver the news. You, too, Ray. We still need photos of the victims once they're removed from the wreck . . ." She paused, her eyes searching Ray's face. "Are you doing okay?"

"Yeah."

"You don't look okay," said Lew. "Ray," she said, dropping her voice, "I have some idea of how you must be feeling right now. The night my son died was the worst of my life. It's one thing when a stranger is murdered—it's quite another when you know the person. Doc said Peg was a close friend of yours . . . maybe you know how I can reach her family?"

She reached over to put her hand on Ray's arm. "Would it help if you're the one to call them?"

"That I cannot do," said Ray, moving away. "Sorry, Chief, I just . . . I can't . . ."

He started back through the trees to the road. Over his shoulder, he said, "If you call the Hugo Garmin main offices in Chicago, the people there should be able to put you in touch with her family. Hugo and his wife are dead but there's a sister."

"Wait . . ." said Lew, astonished. Hurrying to keep up, she said, "Are you saying Peg is one of *the* Garmins? The grocery chain Garmins? That's a huge company."

"Yep—she's an heiress. Or she was before the old man excommunicated her—the sonofabitch."

"Hold on, Ray, this is hard to believe. Peg Garmin is connected to the *Chicago* Garmins?"

"Their fallen angel." His tone was dry.

Lew's eyes caught Osborne's. "Did you know that?"

"No—I'm as stunned as you are." As they scrambled to keep up with Ray, Osborne was sure that he and Lew had to be asking themselves the same question: Known call girl, widow of a mob bag man, mistress of old Doc Westbrook, *and* heir to the Garmin fortune?

"Ray? Ray!" Lew raised her voice, but the khaki shirt had disappeared from view.

"Give him time, Lew," said Osborne.

eight

Of the pike: it is a fish of ambush.

—J. H. Keene, *The Practical Fisherman*

"Here's the stretch where Peg's car was run off the road," said Ray, pointing to variations in a patch of grass growing along the ditch. "And in the sand alongside you can see tread designs from two different vehicles."

"Sure can," said Lew, dropping to one knee for a close look before quickly sketching each of the tread patterns in her notebook.

She glanced up at the two men. "This is handy. May not be official but I'll know the minute I'm back up the road if one of these matches the tires on Peg's car."

With a look of grim satisfaction, she flipped the notebook closed, then walked slowly along the road, studying the grassy section and the numerous footprints that became obvious once you knew where to look. Osborne was relieved that she had decided to back off questioning Ray about the Garmin family—for the moment at least.

"Honestly, Ray," said Osborne. "I don't know how you do it. Nothing about that grass looks all that different to me. It's not as if it's been chewed up or mowed down . . ."

"No-o-o, but it's been disturbed, Doc. Not bent or broken . . . just . . . *disturbed*. When I was driving down this way, my first thought was it looked like deer had been bedding down. Didn't fit. When's the last time you saw deer bedding down this close to a road? So I pulled over to check it out, and that's when I spotted those tread marks."

"And thank goodness you did, Ray," said Lew. "The Wausau boys may do good lab work, but they would never pick up on something so subtle as disturbed grass. I know I wouldn't. And look how much we've accomplished here—from evidence of Peg's car run off to the murder site—"

"Yep. I got photos of every bit of it, too. While the sun was good and high so you'll have the definition you need." He looked at Lew. "If you and Doc are okay with this, shall we drive back up so I can shoot those last few photos that you need? I'll get 'em developed right away. Should have them for you later this evening."

"Thank you, Ray," said Lew. "Oh, man," she said as they trudged toward their vehicles, "at least we've got a start on this."

"Feeling a little overwhelmed?" said Osborne, putting a hand on her shoulder.

"More than a little." Lew gave a pained laugh. "Forget the razzbonyas at Country Fest. Now I've got three murder victims and where do I go from here? Do I assume they all died for the same reason? Or was one the target and the others in the wrong place at the wrong time?"

"Peg was the target," said Ray, his voice flat.

"C'mon, Ray." said Lew. "We don't know that. Just because she was who she was, doesn't mean a thing. We have no proof why any of the three died. Which . . ." Fatigue washed across her face as she paused then said, "Which is why there will be no fishing tonight, tomorrow night— maybe not even the next night. I have to talk to those families—the sooner I know more, the better." She looked hard at Ray.

His features tightened as he said, "I knew Peg—not the family." Slipping into his pickup, he drove off.

Turning the police cruiser around to head back up the road, Lew glanced at Osborne. "Doc, I am so short of manpower—I need Ray's help, but not if he's going to leap to conclusions that could damage the investigation. Until we know what was going on in each one of the women's lives, how can we possibly know why they were murdered?"

"He'll come around," said Osborne. "Right now he's upset."

"You think *he's* upset," said Lew. "I know a few folks who'll be plenty worried when they hear Peg Garmin is dead."

"Oh yes," said Osborne. He could name a few himself. And that wasn't counting the wives.

Lew slowed as they neared the site of the wreck. Ray was already out of his truck and walking toward the area where the bodies were being readied for transport. On seeing his camera, the EMTs backed away. Ray moved slowly around each of the victims, leaving Peg for last. Osborne stood by in case he needed help.

After shooting several photos from a standing position, Ray knelt over Peg's body, camera in his right hand. He brushed the hair back from her face. Startled, he stared down. Then, turning his head to one side, he pressed the fingers of his left hand against his eyelids. The gesture seemed to work: He inhaled deeply and turned back to shoot the close-ups.

When he had finished, he let the camera swing from the strap around his neck and, sitting back on his heels, covered his face with both hands. He stayed there, not moving. Just as Osborne started forward, anxious to help, Ray stood, gave a slight wave to the EMTs, and walked off. He couldn't have gone ten feet when a cloud appeared on the crest of the hill: the van from Channel 12.

Pulling up behind one of the two ambulances parked in front of the tow truck, a stocky figure in tan slacks and a short-sleeved green plaid shirt jumped out, flung open the side door of the van, and leaned in to reach for his equipment. Dave Schoeneck, red-haired and raspy-voiced, worked for a TV station out of Rhinelander that was so small he had to function as cameraman, sound tech and reporter—simultaneously.

He spent so many hours covering high school sports and local social events that anything smacking of real news was heartily appreciated, which explained his behavior at the moment. Arms and elbows flashing, he rushed to load himself down with equipment and sprint across the gravel road, face flushed from the heat.

"Sorry, Dave," said Lew, moving to block his way before he could get past the ambulance. "Until I have a chance to notify the families, I cannot allow the press anywhere near the scene of the accident."

"Oh, so it's an accident?" Dave shouldered the camera as he reached for the switch on his battery pack. He thrust a mike at Lew. "Chief Ferris, are you saying no foul play is involved? We received a call that three women had been found shot to death—"

"All that I can confirm is that we have a traffic fatality on a back road in the township of Loon Lake. No more information will be made available until the family or families of the deceased are informed. Now turn off that camera or you will spend the night in the brand-new Loon Lake jail—do I make myself clear?"

"Sure." Dave gave her a sheepish look. "Had to get something, Chief. I persuaded the news director to let me cover this instead of Shania Twain's bus. Ray Pradt's the one who called and insisted I get out there. I see his truck—is he around?"

Just then he spotted Ray crossing the road toward the pickup. "Hey, guy!" said Dave. "Looks like I'm outta luck. Chief Ferris said no can do on this so-called accident. How 'bout we shoot a quickie on that incident with the smelly fish this morning. That way at least I got *something* for the six o'clock news—where's that hat of yours?"

"Dave, I can't do that right now. I just . . . I can't," said Ray, backing off.

"Don't do this to me," said Dave. "Hell, you're the one got me to drive all the way out here—"

"I—I—" Ray couldn't finish. Tears glistened on his cheeks. He ducked into his truck.

The cameraman watched him, then turned to Lew. "That's a first. You can always rely on that guy for B-roll. Well . . . now—why do I feel something big *is* happening out here?"

Dave took his time unloading his equipment, then climbed into the driver's seat of the van. Lew had walked back to talk to Bruce but Osborne remained nearby, ready to buffer Ray if Dave changed his mind.

Through the rolled-down window of the van, he heard the reporter call in to the station, "Bob, send Rory over to cover Shania Twain. I'm gonna stake out St. Mary's—the morgue. Once the families ID the corpses, we got a story. How big? Not sure yet—but it's weird out here."

Osborne waited to follow the ambulances into town. Lew had asked him to meet her at the morgue, where she would need help with the families once they had identified the victims. Teaming up to interrogate sources and suspects had worked so well in the past that she had come to depend on Osborne's presence. It was yet another reason why she kept him on as a deputy.

"Y'know, Doc, it's not the two of us asking questions," she had said one summer evening as they were wading the Prairie River, "it's the two of us *listening*. I hear answers to my questions—but you hear between the lines. You pick up on answers to questions I haven't asked yet."

Osborne gave silent thanks to this unexpected benefit of his profession. Years of practicing dentistry had taught him the source of a problem might not be in the actual symptom, but in a patient's history or in nearly forgotten details.

"And when you're with me, people tend to open up more easily."

"Oh, come on—that's because they're afraid of dentists," said Osborne, embarrassed by the compliment.

"Hardly," said Lew. "I doubt anyone's afraid of you, Doc. You have such a quiet, reassuring way—you make people feel comfortable. Even a crook responds to kindness and patience."

Osborne was grateful for the darkening sky—she couldn't see him blush. And who knew if it was the hatch two nights later or the lightness in his heart that prompted four brook trout to torpedo his Grizzly Kings.

Ray drove off first, then the emergency vehicles. Osborne pulled onto the road behind them—toward the main highway and in the opposite direction of the clearing.

For a third of a mile, the road continued to run straight, but then it made a sharp ninety-degree turn, following the property line of an old farmstead. Osborne slammed on his brakes and hit Reverse. He backed around the sharp corner for a good look: a windbreak of sturdy oaks. You hit those trees at fifty, sixty miles an hour . . .

nine

Make voyages. Attempt them. There's nothing else.

—Tennessee Williams

Twenty minutes after the EMTs had delivered the three corpses to the morgue at St. Mary's Hospital, Pat Kuzynski's mother arrived. Osborne hadn't seen Pauline Leffterholz since fitting her with a bridge years ago. He had heard that she was widowed for the second time and running her late husband's dog kennel in a hamlet west of Gleason.

Unsteady on her feet, Pauline moved slowly down the narrow hallway, one hand clutching the arm of a man in navy blue shorts—shorts so short they could have been swimming trunks. They *should* have been swimming trunks. Unfortunately they weren't.

As Pauline and her escort neared, Osborne could see that under the brim of his black baseball cap, which was emblazoned with a gold Budweiser logo, were the eyes of a weasel—a weasel who appeared to a good deal younger than Pauline.

Pauline did not look good. Her eyes were dull and sunken, her skin sallow. Where she had once been a pleasant-faced woman with prominent cheekbones, generous cheeks, and a pumpkin-wide smile, now her face was pouched and drooping—ravaged by hard drinking.

Though Osborne was sure she had yet to turn fifty-five, she looked seventy.

"Doc," said Pauline, her voice deep and thick from cigarettes, "how long's this gonna take?"

"I'm not sure, Pauline," said Osborne. "I'll help you through the identification here, then Chief Ferris needs to meet with us over at the Court House."

"Fred . . ." said Pauline, letting go of the man in the short shorts, "I'll meet you at the Elbow Tap later. No reason for you to be stuck here. You take the truck—I'll call the bar when I'm finished."

That worked for the weasel. He gave her quick peck on the cheek and fled.

"Doc?" said another voice, reedy and hesitant. Osborne spun around.

"Ralph," said Osborne, extending a hand to a thin, stooped man dressed in jeans and a faded pink flannel shirt. With the exception of the pink shirt, the rest of Ralph Federer was gray: his hair, his skin, even his worried eyes. "I am so sorry—"

Before Osborne could finish, Ralph pointed at the swinging doors leading into the morgue: "How much you think all this is gonna cost?"

For the second time, Osborne had to admit he didn't know.

What he did know, after a brief but close viewing of the bullet wounds in the heads of the three victims before the two parents arrived, was what had caused Ray to break down as he took that final set of photos: Peg Garmin's face. Her eyes wide open, her teeth clenched. She had seen death coming.

It was after six when the four of them gathered in Lew's office, their chairs spread around the front of her desk with

Osborne seated off to the right. Pauline sat slumped against the arms of her chair while Ralph hunched forward, elbows on his knees, arthritic fingers clutched in a tight ball. He had been the only one to speak up so far. Pauline seemed determined to remain silent, swinging her head like a turtle when someone spoke, her eyes heavy-lidded and sullen.

"Don't ask me," said Ralph, repeating his ignorance of Donna's comings and goings. "I jes dunno, Chief. Since my wife died, Donna's always had her own place, so I don't see too much of her. Alls I know is, she was working at Thunder Bay 'til she could audition at the casino. Called me a couple months ago pretty excited 'cause she got accepted to train to be a dealer up there—at the poker tables. Pays good money, y'know. Health benefits and better tips than she got dancing—"

"From the winners," said Lew. "Losers can get touchy. Think she might have had an opportunity to be around some unhappy losers? Maybe somebody who blamed her for their losses?"

"Like I said—she was still in training," said Ralph. "After that you gotta audition before they let you work the table. So, no, I don't think so."

"Boyfriends? Did she dump anyone recently?"

Ralph shrugged. Short of recognizing his daughter's face, he seemed to know little about her life. From the sound of it, they rarely spoke. Osborne cautioned himself not make the same mistake, to stay in better touch with Mallory. Erin he chatted with daily—but Mallory. . . . Why did he always hang back when it came to his older daughter?

"Anyone with a grudge against *you* who might want to hurt Donna?" said Lew.

"Me! Hell, no," said Ralph. "Ain't got nobody I owe money to. Pay cash for everything. Ain't even got a dog for the neighbors to shoot. What the hell makes you ask me that anyway?"

Pauline's heavy lids had flickered when Lew asked the question of Ralph. Now she propped herself up on one elbow to say, "Ain't nobody mad at me neither. 'Cept two stepkids who think I got all their old man's money when he died two years ago, which I did, but only after nursing him through three years of cancer. Don't think I don't deserve it. But they sure wouldn't take that out on my Patsy . . . would they?"

"Who knows," said Lew. "We have to explore all the possibilities. Pauline, what about Pat—had she been in any trouble recently?"

"Now hold on right there," said Pauline, her tone belligerent. "My Patsy was a good girl." She shook a finger at Lew as she said, "Just 'cause she danced at Thunder Bay is no reason for you to think she was a slut or she did drugs or she gambled—"

"Did I say any of that?" said Lew, returning Pauline's glare.

"You don't have to say it—I know what you're thinking!" The accusation was fierce.

Lew glanced down, aligned some papers on the desk in front of her, then looked up to meet the hostile eyes. "No, Pauline, you don't know what I'm thinking. So let me tell you: I'm thinking that three women were shot to death by an individual who is still at large. How do I find that person? By doing my best to get some questions answered *as soon as possible*.

"Why were these three women in that car together? Where had they been? Where were they going?"

"I got a theory," said Ralph, shaking his head with conviction. "I'll bet we got ourselves a serial killer hangin' out at that damn Country Fest. You wouldn't believe the jabones they got there."

"That's possible, Ralph," said Lew with a respectful nod before turning back to Pauline. "You know my daughter worked her way through her first year of college dancing at Thunder Bay. About eight years ago."

Pauline stared at her, speechless for a second, then said, "Not when the Broomleys owned it?"

"Yep," said Lew. "And *those* were hard people to work for. Did you know them?"

"Oh yeah, b-a-a-d news that pair. Do you know that old lady would steal the girls' tips right off the table before they had a chance to pick 'em up? Used to stop by there once in a while with my first husband, and I tell you I saw her do it. Couldn't believe my own eyes. So you had a kid who worked there, huh. You a cop then?"

"No, I was a secretary over at the mill."

"Oh, I had a lot of friends at the mill up until a few years ago." As Pauline spoke, her face lightened up and ten years dropped away. "Surprised we haven't met—'course I do live way the hell down Highway 17. Can I smoke?"

Lew got up and walked over to open two windows. "Sure."

"Where's your daughter now?" said Pauline, reaching into her purse for a pack of cigarettes and a lighter.

"In the Milwaukee area. She's in the accounting business. I've got two grandchildren." Lew smiled.

"That's nice," said Pauline. "I like hearing that. Patsy was on her way, y'know." She lit her cigarette, sat back, and inhaled deeply. "Yep, she got rid of the creep husband and was planning to enroll at Nicolet College up in Rhinelander—she wanted to do the culinary arts thing."

Pauline paused, turned her head to one side, and covered her eyes with the back of the hand holding the cigarette. She gave a short sob, then sat rigid in her chair. Lew stood to walk around the desk and set a box of Kleenex in her lap. Pauline plucked one and held it to her face.

As Lew returned to her chair, she walked behind Osborne. She tapped him lightly on the shoulder: his turn next.

"It's my fault," said Pauline, her voice muffled by tears and smoke. "I got the money for her to go to school. Why the hell didn't I just give it to her? If she hadn't been working at that damn club, she wouldn't be dead."

"How's that?" said Lew, her voice soft.

"That's how she got in with those two." The bitterness in her tone made it sound like Donna and Peg were up to no good.

"You wait a minute," said Ralph, thrusting his face at Pauline, "my Donna was a good woman. You watch what you say, lady."

"I didn't mean it that way," said Pauline, wiping at her cheeks. "I just meant they wouldn't have all been out together if they hadn't met, and they kinda met because of Thunder Bay."

Lew signaled Osborne with a quick glance.

"Pauline," he said, "what's this about Pat's ex-husband? Was he abusive? Could he be a suspect?" Osborne kept his voice low-key and professional—it was a tone he knew to be effective with patients who were frightened or near hysteria. Once calmed, people were likely to tell him everything he needed to know.

"Well, Butch hated Patsy—that's for sure. She turned him in, y'know. They were living in Point when she found out he was cooking crystal meth in the trunk of his car. Scared her to death. She knew if she didn't turn him in that she'd end up in prison herself—as an accomplice, y'know. That guy was crazy high most of the time."

"Crazy and abusive?" said Osborne.

"He hit her a couple times and, yeah, once he threatened to kill her."

"Last name Kuzynski—what's the first name?" said Lew, pen poised over her notepad.

"I'll get you all the information—he's doing time. Ten years. Patsy was staying at my place so the records ought to be around somewhere."

"Oh," said Lew, setting the pen down. "More likely he would have hired someone to do it for him if that's the case."

"I don't know with what," said Pauline. "He ain't got no money."

"Let's go back to the women for a minute," said Osborne. "Peg Garmin was quite a bit older than both your daughters—by at least twenty, twenty-five years."

"You'd never know it," said Pauline, her voice offering a hint of affection. "That girl was young at heart. I know she . . . well, what she did was her business. The fact is she was a very nice person and helped my Patsy out a lot last year."

"Helped her financially?" said Osborne.

"Oh no, nothing like that. Once they found out they were both going to the same plastic surgeon—way the hell down in Milwaukee—Peg would let Patsy ride down with her. Save on gas, y'know. A coupla times, Peg drove all that way just to pick her up. Well, maybe she had some shopping to do, too. But that's where Patsy first met Peg— in the doc's waiting room."

"How long ago was that?"

"Oh, maybe a year and a half ago."

"And how did Pat know Donna?"

"Oh, they've known each other a long time—they worked together at Thunder Bay?"

As Pauline was speaking, Ralph had edged his chair forward, anxious to interrupt. "Hey, y'know something? I think Donna was seeing that same doctor. She told me that's why she took the job at the club in the first place— so she could pay some medical bills."

"Yeah," said Pauline. "Patsy and Donna both got the same package—breast implants and some Botox. Oh— and their teeth whitened. But Peg had something different done. Went wrong, too. That's why she was driving down there so often."

"Teeth whitened by a plastic surgeon?" said Osborne, making a mental note to check into that. "So what you're telling me is that all three of these women have been seeing the same doctor?" said Osborne. Pauline nodded. "Isn't that rather unusual?"

"Not really," said Pauline. "Everyone at Thunder Bay knows Dr. Forsyth. I think he sends brochures to all the clubs where they got strippers. That's what he does— breast implants, and anything else a girl might need to keep her job. A few of those gals have some years on 'em, doncha know."

The phone on Lew's desk rang. She raised a hand to quiet everyone as she answered, then said she would take the call in a nearby room. "Keep going, Doc, I'll be right back." She hurried out the door.

"So we know how they met. Do you have any idea why they were all three together?" said Osborne.

Ralph shrugged but Pauline gave an eager nod. "Sure— it was karaoke night. Every other Wednesday for the last six months those three been driving down to Wausau to have dinner and go to this bar where they do karaoke."

"Every other Wednesday? Never any other night of the week?"

"Wednesday was Patsy and Donna's night off."

Lew came back into the room and took her seat at the desk. "What did I miss?" At the mention of Wausau and karaoke, she said, "Do we know which club?"

"Oh, they had their favorite—Chucky D's," said Pauline. "And doncha know they had the best time every time. Patsy would tell me. . . ."

Sadness crept across Pauline's rough features as she said, "I hope to hell it wasn't someone from there that killed them. I don't think I could stand knowing that someone who saw my Patsy so happy would—"

"Pauline," said Lew, "from what you've just told us, can we assume that as of Wednesday night, they were alive and on their way to Wausau?"

"On their way *back*," said Pauline. "Patsy always called me as they left so I would unlock the door for her. When you run a business like mine, you don't leave no doors unlocked y'know."

"So what time would that have been?"

"Same as always—one in the morning."

"And then they would drive straight back."

"Yep, one pit stop for gas, have one last drink together—then home."

Osborne looked over at Lew as he said, "And where was that last stop?"

"Oh . . ." Pauline paused and grimaced, "That I don't know. Never asked."

"Jeez," said Ralph. "Must be a hundred places 'tween here and Wausau where you can get gas and a beer at one-thirty in the morning."

"Not if we're lucky," said Lew, standing up.

ten

Within you there is a fire / Within the fire / An expanse of water.

—DoDo Jin Ming, contemporary artist

The wooden sign at the top of the driveway off Wolf Lake Road made Peg Garmin's cottage easy to find. Hung from a wrought-iron pole, it was painted with a lavender and lemon yellow iris whose green tendrils twisted around four words etched in a delicate script: BABE IN THE WOODS.

Osborne pulled his car in behind Lew's cruiser and walked down the asphalt drive. The cottage was situated on the kind of real estate difficult to come by in northern Wisconsin: a level site with a western exposure blessed with sunsets. Tonight the view was spectacular—the lake sparkling with diamonds and promising one of those long, clear summer evenings when the sun refuses to go down.

He paused for a moment to appreciate the quiet loveliness of water and sky. No neighboring homes or cabins invaded the view, which meant that Peg's property had to include a good five hundred feet of shoreline. Five hundred feet on Wolf Lake would sell for thousands of dollars *per foot*. Osborne gave a silent whistle. Whatever else Peg Garmin may have left behind, this land alone had to be worth close to a million.

He found Lew on the porch, about to push open the front door. "Ray was right," she said as she pressed down on the handle and the door swung open. "The place is unlocked." After remembering that Peg rarely locked her doors, Ray had called Lew's office and offered to drive over and secure the cottage—but she had thanked him and said she preferred to do it herself.

Osborne followed her in. They stood for a moment, taking in the details of the living room. The setting sun sent rays of light through a picture window facing west. Dust motes floated in the gold air. All was silent, expectant.

An old oak desk situated to the left of the door held an oval brass bowl into which had been tucked a number of pieces of mail. Also on the desktop were three more items: a blank notepad, a ring-bound weekly calendar, and a small address book, set side by side and in line with the edge of the desk. A tall ceramic mug, painted with a map of Wolf Lake, held pens, pencils, and a pair of scissors.

"Very neat," said Osborne, glancing around the room. The house felt good—warm, welcoming, everything in its place, from pillows on the sofa to newspapers stacked neatly on a side table. It was as if Peg had dusted and vacuumed before she left.

"Peaceful . . . and undisturbed," said Lew. "Certainly doesn't look like anyone's been in here rummaging around, does it. I'd like to do a quick check—see if anything jumps out at us—and come back in the morning for a thorough search.

"And just so you know, Doc, it's legal to look over everything that's out in the open. Anything else has to wait until tomorrow when I'll have that search warrant."

Lew waved toward the far side of the living room where two doors were closed and another, to a bathroom, stood open. "I'll start in here—why don't you check the back entrance and the kitchen area."

Earlier, while Lew completed the paperwork for the warrants that would allow her to do a thorough inspection of each of the victim's homes, Osborne had walked Pauline out to the curb and waited with her until the weasel drove up. She seemed to stand straighter now, and her face was less fallen than when she had arrived. She told Osborne that in spite of her grief, she felt a little better knowing she had been able to give the Loon Lake Police valuable information.

"You certainly pointed Chief Ferris in the right direction, Pauline," said Osborne. "I hope you know you can trust her to follow up on anything else that might come to mind."

"Oh, yes," said Pauline, "I trust her all right—I can tell she's damn good at what she does." Osborne was relieved to hear that. Pauline may have walked in angry and defensive but she was leaving eager to cooperate.

After asking her not to disturb any of her daughter's belongings until they could be examined, Lew had given Pauline her business card—on the back of which she had written both her cell and her home phone numbers. "Anything you think might be important—please call me right away," said Lew, her arm around the woman's shoulders. "Do not hesitate. Understand?"

Pauline had nodded, eyes glimmering with tears.

Ralph got the same card, but without the extra phone numbers. No doubt he would have multiple theories on what had happened to his daughter—input Lew preferred to filter. Marlene would know how to handle him.

"In the meantime," Lew had said, shaking his hand, "I'm going to bring on an extra deputy or two so I can get somebody up to those poker tables where Donna was training. Thanks to you and Pauline, we have some excellent leads here, Ralph."

Before Lew left the office, she touched base with Bruce, who was still hoping to make the Shania Twain performance. He had nothing new to report, except that the overturned convertible had been thoroughly checked for trace evidence and was on its way to Robbie's warehouse. He added that Robbie had been able to reach his friend in Rhinelander and Bruce gave them the go-ahead to pull the car's electronics for a computer analysis first thing in the morning.

Walking to their cars after talking to Bruce, Lew told Osborne that the call that came in while she was questioning Ralph and Pauline was from a security guard at the Hugo Garmin headquarters in Chicago, where she had left a voice message earlier. The guard refused to give out any personal phone numbers, but promised to get the necessary information to "the right people."

"He wouldn't even give me names," said Lew. "Even though I told him it was official police business. Can you believe that? So I gave him all my numbers and asked that the family or someone close to the family call me as soon as they get the news—no matter how late. I made sure he knew to tell them I would have my cell phone with me and, even if I'm out of range, I should be able to return their call within half an hour."

As they arrived at Peg's cottage, Lew was still waiting for the call.

Before walking off toward the kitchen, Osborne took a long look around the spacious living room. One wall held a television with a VCR and DVD player and a stereo system. Shelves along the wall on either side of the TV were laden with CDs and videotapes.

Below the picture window on the west wall was a sofa angled to face two matching armchairs upholstered in gold corduroy. The furniture, including lamps and a coffee table, was arranged on a dark green rug. At one end of the room was a stone fireplace next to which was an ottoman. A folded afghan was draped over one arm of the sofa. The room radiated casual comfort—but yet, something was missing. Osborne puzzled for a moment, then gave a shrug and set off to check the rest of the house.

The kitchen faced east. It was a long, narrow room with appliances along the inside wall and a small round table with two chairs nestled into a nook, with floor-to-ceiling windows on the far end. Osborne looked through the windows: Peg had a morning view of the lake, too. She must have loved the place.

On one counter, below a wall phone, was an answering machine, its red light blinking. A quick check of the cupboards, which had glass fronts, disclosed stacks of dishes and glassware, a bar set for mixing martinis, and six bags of chocolate chip cookies. A pantry held cereal boxes, some canned soups, and a few baking supplies. Everything was so neat, he was surprised the soups were not in alphabetical order.

Osborne opened the refrigerator. At least a dozen bottles of beer—all different brands but each brand lined up one after the other, along with tonic water and sodas—filled three shelves. A selection of cheeses and a bowl of fresh limes were packed into the crisper. The overhead freezer opened to display boxes of frozen meals—all Weight Watchers brand.

The kitchen of a single woman who entertained.

"Hey, Doc," said Lew, calling from the front of the

house, "come here—tell me what you think of this stuff . . ."

He found her in the bathroom examining the contents of a tall white cabinet with glass doors. Four of its five shelves held neatly arranged bathroom appliances—blow dryers, a basket of curlers, a curling iron—along with an assortment of cosmetics and perfumes. The top shelf held bottles of aspirin and Advil, several cold remedies, and several vials from a pharmacy. Osborne could identify the contents of the prescription drug containers through the glass.

"Painkillers," he said, pointing to two. Of the remaining two, he said, "This one is a decongestant—and this a medication for dizziness."

"The dates are all pretty recent," said Lew.

"She had an infection of some kind. Must be related to the plastic surgery since the prescribing physician listed on these is Forsyth."

"I saw that," said Lew. "Interesting, isn't it. If we didn't know better, we might assume she had been having dizzy spells, which could cause her to lose control of her car . . . right?"

"I would give it serious thought after seeing all this medication," said Osborne.

The first of the two closed doors in the living room opened to a light, airy room, which seemed smaller than it was due to its occupant: a large brass bed. The bed was covered with a cheery yellow, white, red, and spring green patterned quilt that, along with a tumble of colorful pillows, lit up the space. The quilt matched the curtains, which were pulled to let in the western light.

Alongside the bed was a lamp table laden with magazines and a paperback novel. Nearby was an antique dressing table and matching mirror. Bottles of perfume and makeup were set in a row across the top of the dressing table. A handsome cherry dresser stood against one wall.

"Compulsively neat," said Lew.

"Wait 'til you see the kitchen," said Osborne. He took a long, slow look around the room. "Lew, I can't put my finger on it—but I feel like something is missing. I felt it in the living room, I feel it here . . ."

"Really?" Lew gave him a thoughtful look.

The door to the second bedroom opened to darkness. The room smelled of mothballs with a hint of what Osborne imagined to be stale sex. Lew flicked the light switch. Brown and tan striped curtains were pulled closed. The curtains matched the bedspread on the queen-sized bed, which had a simple oak headboard. Cabinet-style tables on each side of the bed held lamps with light brown shades. Otherwise, the tables were empty. No books, no magazines, no ashtrays, no coasters.

A tall wooden wardrobe stood against one wall, one door ajar. Except for half a dozen suit hangers, it was empty. Directly across from the bed, resting on a wooden trestle table, was a flat-screen TV with a built-in VCR and DVD player. A chest of drawers was angled into the remaining corner of the room.

"I wonder if she gets to write this off as her home office," said Lew in a wry tone. She reached for the cell phone that hung from her belt and checked it.

"Do you have service here?" said Osborne.

"Yes, funny they haven't called yet." She looked around the room, "I'm hesitant to open drawers until I have that search warrant . . ."

Osborne walked around the queen-size bed and out of instinct bent to close a half-open door to the cabinet under one of the lamps, only to have a stack of magazines slide onto the floor. The kind of magazines that were masked on the highest racks and sold bagged at the convenience store.

"Doc, wait—let me pick those up," said Lew, holding out her gloved hands, "In case I need them checked for prints."

"Wait," said Osborne as she came around the bed. He put a hand on her arm to stop her as he pointed to the floor. Where the magazines had slid near the bed was a long white box, its length visible just below the bedspread. "Does that qualify as being 'in plain sight'?"

Lew didn't answer. She knelt to pull the box forward. It was an unusual size. Osborne guessed it to be about sixteen inches by twelve inches and three inches deep—and made of a heavy-weight cardboard. Across the top of the box, scrawled in black marker and printed in capital letters was the phrase: PICTURES OF PEOPLE WHO HURT PEOPLE.

eleven

In wildness is the preservation of the world.

—Henry David Thoreau

"Pictures." Osborne snapped his fingers. Lew looked up from where she was leaning over the unopened box.

"That's it," he said. "I *knew* something was bothering me as I walked through these rooms. The woman has nothing on her walls. No pictures, no photos, no paintings—nothing."

"Are you sure?" said Lew, her eyes questioning. She moved past him into the living room. He followed, watching as she scanned the walls in that room, the front bedroom, and the kitchen. "That *is* odd, Doc. You and I have family photos sitting out all over the place. Too many in my case, that's for sure.

"Even here," said Lew, pointing in amazement from where she stood in the middle of the kitchen. "Now when was the last time you saw a refrigerator door that didn't have something stuck on it with a magnet? Reminders, postcards, the little things that bring back memories . . ."

"Memories—that's a good way to put it," said Osborne.

He had to admit that he was extreme himself when it came to personal photos. Framed pictures of his daughters at every age could be found throughout his house. Heck, he had one whole photo album devoted to pictures of his buddies from the deer shack. Thirty years of overserved men in long underwear and crummy beards? Mary Lee had found that collection disgusting. But he loved to page through—it brought back all the fun.

"Doc, to me memories mean family," said Lew. "And while this house feels lived in, I don't get a sense of family." She grimaced. "Makes me not want to open that box."

As he followed Lew back to the bedroom where the box was waiting on the bed, he thought of the Peg he had known in the days when she was a patient: the perfect porcelain skin, the coiffed and sprayed blond hair—and her eyes. Those eyes that always looked away so quickly, that refused to hold his gaze. Eyes that would stare down while he spoke. He always felt bad when she left the office: What he had done to frighten her?

"No sense of family." Osborne repeated the phrase, thrusting his hands into his pockets as he followed her back through the house. "But maybe, given what we know about Peg—maybe that shouldn't surprise us."

"Well, let's see what we have here, Doc," said Lew, sounding resigned and not a little worried as she sat down on the bed, the box in her lap. " 'Pictures of people who hurt people,' " she read the message again. Before lifting the lid, she glanced up at Osborne. "Don't let me forget to look through the mail on the desk before we leave—see if there's anything with her handwriting on it. Be nice to know if she's the one who wrote this."

The box was packed with loose photos. Dozens and dozens, color, black and white, all different sizes—some were tiny, so old that their edges were pinked and curling. Lew gave the box a quick shake that exposed a .38-caliber revolver in a worn holster and a badge. "Thought it seemed a little heavy on one end."

She set the gun and the badge on the table beside the bed. "That's probably her husband's gun and police badge," said Lew. "I never met the man but I sure heard about him: Frank McNulty, ex-cop, convicted felon."

"But a nice enough guy," said Osborne. "Good fisherman. Muskie—he loved to fish muskie."

Almost everyone in Osborne's circle of friends knew Frank. And why Peg Garmin never took her husband's name, though they had arrived in Loon Lake twenty years earlier as a married couple. Multiple versions had been told of the escapades that drove them north. But whatever story was heard, listeners would agree that it was a wise decision of Peg's to remain Garmin, not McNulty.

He had been a street cop and she was a prostitute when they met in Chicago. Once Peg married Frank, she left the business, but that didn't make Frank a hero. He was a bagman for the mob. And took the fall for his bosses. He did time in Marion, never ratted, and when he got out, he got paid. So he and Peg drove north to Loon Lake, where they put all that money down on a small resort on Scattering Rice Lake.

They had a knack for the resort business. They hired a chef who could grill a terrific New York strip while the couple shared the bartending. At first people came out of curiosity, only to find a husband and wife whose notoriety was hard to believe given their open, friendly demeanors. Frank was an encyclopedia when it came to fishing muskie. Peg had a natural sweetness that made her a good listener—not to mention being easy on the eyes.

Within two years, the bar and the supper club were thriving. Osborne and his fishing buddies were among many of the locals who got in the habit of stopping by Deer Haven for a "Leinie" or two or three after a good night's fishing. And nearly every time he stopped in, Osborne would give a wave down the bar to another couple of regulars: Herb and Helen Pradt—Ray's parents.

One day, Frank dropped dead. He was only forty-seven. Peg had to sell the resort, and soon after she was selling herself. The first few years after Frank's death, she went kind of crazy. The town traded stories of angry wives storming into her apartment, of binge drinking, of local merchants' bills going unpaid. Even Osborne had to turn her account over to a collection agency.

But then she settled down. She gave up the constant hustling and appeared to be happy with one well-to-do client. Well, everyone knew there might be another guy every now and then—but she seemed happy with Harold.

Osborne was only acquainted with the man. Harold Westbrook had retired from a medical practice in Milwaukee, where he had been an orthopedic surgeon. His wife of many years passed away shortly after they moved into a handsome brick home in Loon Lake, which was where she had grown up. To everyone's surprise, Harold chose to stay in town. But they had no children and he loved to fly-fish.

He was a tall man, surprisingly agile for his years and quite good-looking with craggy features under a thatch of stark white hair. Mary Lee had often commented to Osborne that she hoped he would look as good as Harold as he aged. Whenever she said that, Osborne resisted giving her a dim eye. What would be the benefit? She hadn't shared a bedroom with him for twenty years. Was she planning to start in their seventies?

But it was the baby blue convertible parked for hours in front of his house that made Harold a legend. The early-morning coffee crowd at McDonald's might snicker when

Peg and Harold's names were mentioned in tandem—but it was only out of envy. More than one guy mulling over his black coffee would look a little wistful, as if he wouldn't mind having a reputation for bad behavior at the age of eighty.

Lew tipped the remaining contents of the box onto the bedspread. At first glance, the photos were typical of family albums: individuals posing for the camera, family gatherings, first communions, weddings. Innocent photos.

"Look at this," said Lew, holding out a black-and-white print of a pudgy little girl in a pouf of a white tulle dress that was tied high on her chest with a silk bow.

The baby ballerina was smiling for the camera, her arms reaching up. One hand held a long stick with a tulle pompom trailing a silk ribbon on one end; the fingers of her other hand were spread wide in a happy wave. She had short, straight hair that was brushed back and secured to the top of her head with another white bow. The child was barefoot—caught on her tiptoes in an exuberant leap.

"Now that is one cute kid," said Lew. She turned the photo over and read the back: "Margaret at age three."

"That has to be Peg," said Osborne. He handed the photo back to Lew, who was shuffling through the rest of the photos. She reached for a square, buff-colored envelope with four words scrawled across it: *Peg O'My Heart.*

The envelope was unsealed. It contained one black-and-white photo. Lew groaned as she held it so Osborne could see it, too. He looked—then looked away. It was as if a spider, black and horrid, had crawled out from the envelope.

"Taken by a medical examiner or a coroner," said Lew. "Documenting the assault."

"Do you think it's the same child?" Osborne knew the answer before he asked.

Lew read notations jotted on the back of the picture. "She's identified as Mary Margaret Garmin. Age seven. Offender unknown. Found by her mother in the family pool house."

"Age seven," said Osborne, shaking his head. "Lew, the rage I have for people who do this—"

"Doc, it is the worst part of my job. Believe me." She gave a deep sigh as she slipped the photo back into the envelope. "Could explain a few things, I suppose," said Lew. "Not that this has anything to do with her death."

"I'd like to know who gave her the picture—and who wrote those words. That's nasty."

"And *when* she got it," said Lew. "That envelope was right on top when I opened the box—before I tipped everything out."

"Something else, Lew," said Osborne. "I spotted the box because it was so close to the edge of the bed—as if Peg might have been interrupted while shoving it back under so it wasn't hidden all the way."

"Or someone else was interrupted while trying to hide it."

twelve

If a man is truly blessed, he returns home from fishing to
be greeted by the best catch of his life.

—An unknown wife, somewhere

"Wait—I recognize the name on that return address,"
said Osborne, laying his hand over Lew's as she fanned the
assortment of envelopes across the top of the desk. Most of
the letters that had been stuffed into the brass container appeared to be bills. "Dr. Gerald Rasmussen. He's an oral
surgeon. We've met."

As he scanned the letter, Lew sorted through the remaining pieces of mail.

"Well, this is interesting," said Osborne. "Looks like
Gerry Rasmussen was giving her a second opinion on the
results of some surgery . . . and he mentions his fee for appearing as an expert witness in a trial . . . apparently she
was considering a lawsuit of some kind."

"Against her plastic surgeon, perhaps?" said Lew.

"Could be. Rasmussen does more than oral surgery—
he's also a maxillofacial guy. Excellent reputation. If
you'd like, I'll give him a call in the morning, see what this
is all about?"

"Thank you, Doc, that would be very helpful. I was
hoping you would have the time to sit down with Dr. West-

brook, too. One on one. He might open up better if I'm not there. But do you have the time?"

"I do, but speaking of time, Lew—you have got to take some time off. I'll be happy to do whatever you need so long as the minute this weather cools down, we can get in some time in the water. I know July fishing isn't the best— but you need a break."

"I wish," said Lew, fatigue washing over her face. "I have to admit I'm feeling a little overwhelmed at the moment. Oh, say . . . what's this?" She pulled a piece of notebook paper, edges ripped, from a small white envelope. "This was tucked way in the back behind some credit card offers." She gave it a quick read then handed it to Osborne.

Whoever scribbled the note had such poor penmanship that he could barely make out the words: *Dear Margaret,* it began. *I don't know what to say. I don't know how to do this. Christopher.* That was it. The rest of the page was blank.

Lew checked the envelope. "No return address. Postmark shows it was mailed three weeks ago—from Evanston, Illinois. Christopher, huh. Now there's someone I'd like to talk to. And I'll hold on to both these pieces of mail until we know more."

"Anything else you want to see before we leave?" said Osborne. Lew looked so tired, he hoped she would call it a day. He checked his watch—it was after nine.

"I wish those Garmin people would call," she said, flipping the pages of the address book that had been set so carefully on the desk. "I'm hesitant to contact any of the names in here—could be family, could be a client . . ."

"Why don't you let me take that address book and run some names past Ray to see if any sound familiar. Remember, he's known Peg since he was a kid."

"Let's do that right now," said Lew. "I'm very concerned about our friend. Much as I need his help right now, I'm worried he may be too emotionally invested in this case. I can't have him involved if he's likely to come down too hard on someone—"

"I have the same worry, Lew. He was so upset this afternoon. Are you sure you're up to it tonight?"

"You know me, Doc. Just as soon sort it out right now and get things moving. Or not moving . . ."

Her cell phone rang. It was the dispatcher on the switchboard with news of a traffic accident on the road leading into Country Fest. "Okay," said Lew, sounding defeated, "I'll call Roger and get him out there right away. Any calls for me from Chicago? Darn," she said, disappointed. After signing off with the dispatcher, she checked her phone log to be sure a call hadn't come in while she was talking.

"Isn't Roger suspended for another week?" said Osborne.

"Not anymore he isn't," said Lew with a grim smile. Roger was the deputy she had inherited when she was promoted—a former insurance agent who had tired of forty-hour weeks and joined the police force thinking he could while away his days emptying parking meters until qualifying for an early retirement and a good pension.

But the day Lewellyn Ferris became Chief of the Loon Lake Police Department, Roger's life changed. Unlike her predecessors, she refused to close or set aside a case until she was positive an investigation was complete. She insisted that an officer be present at the site of all traffic accidents, break-ins, and other types of disturbances—*and* write up a detailed report. To his surprise, Roger found himself working. Hard.

Worse than Roger's allergy to hard work was his talent for narrow-minded thinking. Too many times, Lew had had to scold him for being "a bullet head" and send him back into the field with a list of questions. His most recent exercise in poor judgment had devastated the department's budget—not to mention generated a series of jokes aired on local radio stations.

On spotting a beat-up suitcase set out in front of the Loon Lake Union High School during his daily check of the school parking lot, Roger leaped to the conclusion that it was bomb. Lew was in court that morning, her cell phone turned off as ordered by the judge, or she might have been able to prevent his call to the nearest bomb squad—in Milwaukee! One helicopter, six men, and twenty-two thousand dollars later, the suitcase turned out to be nothing more than a moldy prop once used in a school play and set out by the janitor to be taken to the dump.

Lew handled her frustration with the well-meaning deputy by arranging to have him out of her sight for four weeks—suspended with pay.

"Oh, oh, Lew, wait just a minute," said Osborne as she was about to close and lock the front door. "The phone machine in the kitchen was blinking. Do you want to check it before we leave?"

It held one message. A woman's voice, husky and relaxed, said, "Hey . . . are you there? It's me. Peg." It was difficult to tell if the last word was a declaration or a question. Lew replayed it three times and they still could not tell.

"You may think I'm crazy but that sounds like Peg," said Osborne. "But why would she be calling herself?"

"Could be she was trying to reach someone who was waiting for her—here."

Ray's truck was in his drive and his dogs yelped happily at the sound of Osborne and Lew's footsteps—but there was

no Ray. No lights in his trailer. No figure on the dock
bench. No boat.

"Any idea where he might be?" said Lew, standing on
the dock beside Osborne.

"I have a hunch," said Osborne. "Could be wrong. But
it's a ten-minute bet—want to take a boat ride?"

"That I could use."

Within minutes, they were climbing into Osborne's
boat. The dying sun caught cloud banks overhead to throw
pink, purple, coral, and orange in ripples across the water.
The air was orange against the black silhouette of the far
shore.

"What a beautiful evening," said Lew, settling herself
near the prow of Osborne's Alumacraft. He spun the shore
station wheel, lowering the craft so quietly that two ducks,
black against the hot peach of the water, glided by without
a ruffle or a squawk.

With an easy yank of the cord, the 10-horsepower Mercury purred awake. The boat swerved north, and with a
low roar as he kicked up the speed, they were heading for
the first of the channels linking the five lakes that made up
the Loon Lake chain. The rush of air was humid but cool
against their faces. As Lew turned sideways to watch the
shoreline, the wind blew back the open collar of her shirt.

"You don't mind, do you?" she said with that look in
her eye that always undid him as she unbuttoned two more
buttons so the cool breeze could travel across her breasts.
She tipped her head back to let her hair blow in the wind.
"Oooh . . . this feels so good."

"Lewellyn, don't do this to an old man," said Osborne
with a chuckle. She winked in return.

That's when he knew what he had to do sometime over
the next few weeks: find a winter escape that might appeal
to her. Maybe some fly-fishing for saltwater trophies off

the Florida Keys? She refused to take her vacation during the hectic summer months—but she needed a break.

Tomorrow, he decided. He would stop by Erin's house and ask her for advice on the best approach—after all, if he and Lew spent occasional nights together—why not a full week? Maybe two?

The thought banished any feeling of fatigue; he had a plan. And so he drove the boat with one eye on the upcoming channel, the other on the woman he found as spectacular as the sunset.

thirteen

. . . the good of having wisely invested so much time in wild country . . .

—Henry Middleton, *Rivers of Memory*

It was along the ribbon of water between Third and Fourth Lakes, known to locals as the Loon River, where Osborne was sure he would find Ray. No cottages or homes marred this mile-long expanse of pristine vistas protected by wetlands bordering both sides.

Half a mile up was a hole, difficult to locate and known to only a few fishermen: a final resting place of virgin timbers sunk during the lumber rush of the late 1800s—fine underwater structure for predators of a trophy size. The beauty of the place always took Osborne's breath away even as it explained his friendship with a man nearly thirty years his junior and who would rather fish than make a buck.

Every time they approached by boat, Ray would turn to Osborne and utter one word: "sacred." And every time Osborne would nod in return. Not another word was necessary.

"You're sworn to secrecy, Lew," said Osborne, his voice low as he slowed the outboard motor before rounding the bend just ahead.

"C'mon, Doc," said Lew, busy buttoning her shirt, "you know better than that."

He cut the engine and lifted the prop up and out of the water. The boat rocked gently in the wake. They drifted in silence. His eyes adjusted to the dark; Osborne could see the expression on Lew's face and knew what she was thinking.

"The eloquence of quiet water," he said in a whisper.

"Did you make that up?" she whispered back.

"N-o-o-o. Have to credit our favorite razzbonya."

When the boat was still, he reached for the oars. He looked up. The clouds had vanished, unveiling a universe of stars. Dipping the oars one at a time, he pulled the boat around the bend. Then he let it drift.

Off to the right, about fifteen feet from the tamaracks crowding the shore, was a large dark mass, barely visible in the shadows. As they drifted toward the darkness, moonlight spilled from behind the trees to illuminate Ray, eyes closed as he leaned back, sitting high in his chair at the front of the long, flat bassboat. His arms were folded, his legs extended and crossed at the ankles.

"Yo . . ." said Ray without opening his eyes. He sounded as if he had been expecting them.

"Are you okay?" said Lew. Osborne dipped the oars to keep his boat from bumping Ray's.

"Oh yeah," said Ray a little too quickly. He turned his head away as he spoke.

No, you're not, thought Osborne. The water lapped. Somewhere off on Third Lake a loon called.

"Do you want us to leave?" said Osborne.

"No, it's okay. I've been here awhile," said Ray. "Good place for thinking. For looking and listening and thinking. Moon's two nights short of full—did you notice?"

"I've got a few leads," said Lew, trying to sound upbeat. Very quickly she told him what they had learned from

Ralph and Pauline, as well as discovering the letter that indicated Peg was involved in a lawsuit and the cryptic note from someone named Christopher. What she did not mention was the awful photo.

"But no luck reaching Peg's family," she said. "I guess . . . well, since it seems you knew her pretty well. We found an address book at her house, but not knowing who's who—I thought maybe you could help."

"I'll try." Ray opened his eyes but didn't move.

"You said she was a good friend of your mother's . . ." said Osborne.

"Right."

"How did they . . . what I mean is—"

"What you mean is how could a doctor's wife have become such good friends with a high-priced hooker?"

"Thank you—but I wouldn't have put it quite that way."

Ray shrugged. "Doesn't matter. They met one night after my folks had been out fishing, caught two muskies, and decided to celebrate with dinner at Deer Haven. This was right after Peg and Frank had opened their place. Peg was tending bar that night and I guess she and my mom just hit it off right away . . ." He paused.

Osborne and Lew waited, their boat rocking gently over the black water. The loon called again but the haunting cry went unanswered.

Ray untangled his legs and leaned forward to rest his forearms on his knees. He dropped his head for a moment, then raised it as he spoke. "I hated her at first. Hated her. I was fourteen, I guess, when she started stopping by our house in the afternoons. The two of them would sit in the living room and talk for hours. I saw her as one more excuse for my mother to drink, y'know.

"But she wasn't. She . . ." Ray took a deep breath. "She

showed me a way to love my mother." His voice sounded unnaturally high.

"Ray, if this is too hard—" said Lew.

"No, no. It's okay. Better you know the whole story. Doc knows some of it—my mother was a raging alcoholic. 'Two-case Helen' they called her. That's how much booze she would order almost every week. My father wasn't around much during the day. If he wasn't in the office or at the hospital, he was gone fishing, hunting, you name it.

"So when Peg came by our house, I thought she was just another excuse for my mom to sit around and get drunk. She—I mean Peg—knew that's what I was thinking, too.

"Then one afternoon, I was mowing the yard and Peg came out and asked me to stop. She had me sit down on the porch steps with her. Then she asked me how my mother behaved when she was at her worst. Straight out, y'know. It was the way she looked me in the eye and she was so . . . *kind* that I just emptied my heart out. I cried, I told her everything."

Ray paused, rubbed his face with both hands, then continued, "Life in our house wasn't easy. My older brother and sister were already away at college, so I was there by myself. Late at night I would hear my mother screaming, accusing my father of terrible things. I would lie in bed and listen. Christmas was the worst—every Christmas Eve it started and she would be dead drunk through the holidays. And always these accusations that I knew weren't true.

"I was so surprised when Peg—I called her 'Mary Margaret,' by the way. That was her full name though she never used it. I've always thought it was as pretty as she was. I was so surprised when she asked me that that afternoon, I spilled my guts. Told her everything.

"When I finished, she said that I was old enough to know the truth. And in a very simple, direct way she told me that the reason she and my mother had become close friends was because they had been through some things that most people wouldn't understand. That when they were young girls, they had been hurt by other people: they had been 'broken.' That's the word she used. *Broken.*

"I asked her how she knew that about my mom and she said that one night around the bar at Deer Haven, my mother had said something in a certain way—and Peg knew. 'Maybe it's intuition,' she told me, 'but people like us pick up on it in one another pretty quickly.'

"Then Peg told me that she was adopted and that when she was six her adoptive father began abusing her sexually—but no one believed her. Even when she had to go to the hospital, her mother refused to acknowledge what was going on.

"Well, same for my mom. Only she wasn't adopted. She was the oldest girl in a large family. Her father was a religious fanatic. She had the same thing happen to her. Her mother died without ever admitting to Helen that she knew what was going on. That explained to me why my mother had nothing to do with my grandparents.

"Then Peg told me that people cope in different ways. 'When you're broken,' she said, 'you can't be fixed—but you have to go on. So you find a way.' Her way was to become promiscuous to an extreme, but she hoped that she was past all that now that she had found Frank. Whatever bad things Frank McNulty did, when it came to Peg, he was a saint. He cherished her.

"She said my mother used alcohol to take care of herself. She also said that she could see that in spite of my mother's drinking, my parents loved each other." Ray's voice quavered.

"That talk on the porch steps changed my life. From that day on, I looked at my mother differently. I began to pay more attention to when she was sober and see what a good mom she was then. I was able to stop hating her. I could see how my dad, in his way, knew how to help her. That's why when she was so, so drunk and all those terrible memories and emotions would kick in—he would just sit and listen."

Ray shifted in his chair, leaning back again and crossing his arms. "So . . . that's what Peg did for me. I have loved her as a sister, maybe even a surrogate mother over all these years.

"That's it, Chief. That's why I am . . . deter-r-r-mined . . . to find the fiend who murdered those three women."

On hearing those words spoken in the familiar Ray Pradt fashion of emphasis by elongation, Osborne felt relief: The old Ray was back.

"Well . . ." said Lew, hesitating. "That worries me. Don't get me wrong—I need help. I'm only one person and all I have for backup are Todd and Roger. I don't have to tell you and Doc that the Loon Lake Police Department was stretched to the limit *before* this happened, but Ray, if you are intent on revenge, then I can't—"

"Did I say 'revenge'?"

"Sure sounded like it," said Lew.

"Not revenge—*acknowledgment*. I want whoever murdered Mary Margaret Garmin and her friends to acknowledge what they did—to admit their guilt, to be held responsible. Now . . ." said Ray, raising both hands, "I admit I bend the law when it comes to smoking a joint or poaching a bluegill or two, but I will not jeopardize this case in *any* way. Believe me, Chief, I want to see whoever did this in prison."

"Well . . ." Lew sounded doubtful.

"And I hope you don't mind, but I made a phone call already to someone who is going to help us out in a big way—help *you*, I mean. I've asked Gina Palmer to come up from Chicago and—"

"Ray, stop right there," said Lew, sounding frustrated. "I appreciate your effort, but I don't have the budget to pay her. I have barely enough to pay you and Doc. The bill from the Wausau boys alone will force me to go to the city council and the mayor for emergency funding—"

"Let me finish, Chief, please," said Ray. "First, I'm doing this for free. For Mary Margaret. Under no circumstances will I accept a dime. Second, Gina and I barter: I take care of her cottage and she helps me out when I need it. She's already agreed to work on this. I pick her up at the Rhinelander airport tomorrow afternoon."

"Oh . . ." said Lew, dropping her head in thought. "And what have you told her so far?"

"I gave her the details and said that I'm ninety-nine percent sure that Peg was the target. All those goombahs from Frank's past? I'll bet you anything she knew something about somebody who's still alive. Just a few months ago, she told me she'd had some phone calls she didn't appreciate. Two mob types who bought property up in Eagle River ran into her by accident at the grocery store. They wanted to socialize, which she did not appreciate. I figure we start there.

"So Gina is searching the archives at the *Chicago Sun-Times* and the *Tribune* to check for the stories from when Frank was convicted. She'll run those by a couple reporters who cover the mob and see if they know who might still be around from those days.

"Also, she said to tell you that she can do public records searches on each of the women and on any suspects. You know from when she helped out last year that she's a wizard on the Internet. So how's that sound? She's prepared to be here all week."

"Whoa." Lew sounded relieved. "Ray, I gotta hand it to you. You do finagle the darndest things. Okay, you're on but"—she waved a finger at him—"I want you working hand in hand with Doc. He takes better notes than you do, and I want to be sure anything you find can stand up in court."

"Plus you won't worry about me blowing someone's head off."

"Well . . . that, too . . . frankly," she chuckled. "Now will you follow us back to Doc's? I know it's late, but I would love for you to take a quick look at Peg's address book before I head home."

"Sure. Oh, wait, folks, there's one thing I have to do in memory of my friend. I always took her fishing on her birthday—always brought her to this pool. And she always insisted on fishing with a Boogie lure that had been one of Frank's favorites for walleye. A blue one—same color as her car. I rigged up just before you two arrived, planning to make a few casts."

"Little warm for fishing tonight," said Lew.

"True," said Ray. "But those tamaracks throw quite a bit of shade during the day. Who knows? One of the big girls might be down there just waiting for groceries to be delivered."

Osborne was surprised to see Ray pull up a muskie rod. "You're using that with the Boogie?" he said. "That lure's a little small for muskies."

"Yes, it is—but it's Frank's old rod," said Ray, grasping the handle with both hands. "Peg had me keep it with my gear and this is how she always wanted to do it. Of course," he said, smiling for the first time since they had arrived, "she never even got a follow."

• • •

It was the vibrations of the plug that did it. At least that was the verdict delivered by half the McDonald's crowd. The other half voted for the Garcia Ambassador reel, Series 6500, which was the only reason the handle didn't snap out of Ray's hand. Whatever it was, the next ninety seconds on the Loon River that starry night were the stuff of which magnificent fish tales are made.

The blue Boogie hit the surface and dropped to hook one of the submerged logs. Or the bottom of the lake. That was Ray's first thought.

Not Lew's. "Set the hook!" she cried, jumping to her feet and nearly falling out of the boat.

"I did, I did!" Now Ray was on his feet—the muskie rod bent in half for a long, long minute. Osborne held his breath as he watched, knowing Ray never used his drag when fighting a fish. He would tighten it until his line was close to breaking, and once he had a fish on, he would push the reel button and let that fish run.

Tonight, the instant he hit that button, the muskie came out of the water. Fifty inches of sleek, fierce fish, its back long and black, moonlight flashing off its golden-olive flanks. It flew at the boat with such speed that Ray never had a chance to reel in the slack. Another flip into the air, a flash of the undershot jaw with the wicked teeth that looked as though it might swallow Ray—boat and all.

Then it was gone—the line snapped and the blue Boogie on its way to a place dark, deep, and out of the reach of humans.

All was quiet on the Loon River.

"I do believe that was a sign," said Ray, watching the last ripple fade into the night. "I do believe my friend is safe."

fourteen

In the morning be first up, and in the evening last to go to bed, for they that sleep catch no fish.

—English proverb

"C'mon, now," said Osborne, backing away from the open refrigerator with raspberries in one hand and cream in the other, "Erin and the kids picked these this morning—no one leaves until they're gone."

He got no argument from the two people seated at his kitchen table. Not even when he insisted they use cream and a dusting of sugar.

"Umm . . ." said Lew, savoring her first spoonful, "life doesn't get much better than this." She looked more relaxed than she had all day.

It helped that once they were through the last channel back to Loon Lake and out of the sheltering pines, she was able to pick up a voice mail on her cell phone from Peg Garmin's brother-in-law. He left a message that he could be reached at a number in Boulder Junction. Returning the call immediately, Lew made arrangements to meet with the couple, Joan and Parker Nehlson, at nine the next morning.

"He said his wife was too upset to make the call herself even though, given Peg's history, they always expected something like this might happen." Lew spoke between mouthfuls. "These are delicious, Doc, thank you."

"Oh, so it's Peg's fault she was murdered," said Ray. "I like these people already."

"Ray, that is exactly what I don't want to hear from you," said Lew, shaking her spoon at him. "Don't jump to conclusions. I got enough trouble with Roger on that score."

"Sorry," said Ray. "I guess . . . I can understand how they might feel that way." Osborne and Lew stared at him. "No, I do. Really."

"Interesting they called from Boulder Junction," said Lew as she finished the last of her raspberries and held the bowl out for more. "Must be a second home. Ray, see an Illinois address for them? Any names in there look familiar to you?"

Ray had been eating berries with one hand and paging through Peg's address book with the other. "The Nehlsons have an address in Kenilworth—but nothing in Boulder Junction. Maybe they're staying at a resort or with friends. This book is pretty dog-eared. Quite a few names are crossed out."

"Anyone named Christopher?"

"Not yet. Y'know," said Ray, looking up, "you should turn this over to Gina—she can track these people down."

With an approving shake of her head since she had a mouthful of berries and cream, Lew waved her spoon at Ray, "Did Doc tell you what he saw this afternoon—after you left?"

"Oh right, Ray? Maybe you noticed this, too," said Osborne. "I decided to take the south route down the old highway when I was ready to head back to town, and less than a quarter of a mile from where Peg's car was found, the road takes a *sharp* ninety-degree turn. I drove back and forth a couple times and I have to tell you—I think some-one intended for that car to go straight into the pines at the curve. I don't think it was supposed to roll the way it did."

Ray looked at him dumbfounded. "I know exactly where you mean, Doc. Never dawned on me but that makes sense. Be interesting to see what Robbie Mikkleson and his buddy turn up when they check the data recorder from the car."

Lew got up to set her bowl in the sink. She turned to face Osborne and Ray. Leaning back against the counter, she crossed her arms as she said, "About tomorrow. Doc, would you call Dr. Westbrook and see how soon you can meet with him?"

Before Osborne could answer, Ray looked up as he turned the last page of the address book. "Just so you know—Harold Westbrook isn't listed in here."

"That tells us something," said Lew. "Like maybe she kept business separate from personal."

Ray rapped the spine of the little book lightly on the table as he said, "She saw a lot of old Harold over the last year or so. I don't know that I heard she was seeing any-one else. Not like she did a few years back."

"When was the last time you saw her?" said Lew.

"End of June—on her birthday. But we never talked about . . . her self-employment opportunities." Ray gave a sad smile. "That was not the Mary Margaret that I knew—or wanted to know."

"Hmm," said Lew, looking preoccupied. "Another thing—I have got to get up to the casino. Follow up on Donna and that poker business. You never know—could be someone from up there just as easy as a creep from Frank's past." She raised her eyebrows in exasperation. "I hope to hell I can get my arms around this case pretty darn soon. Too many leads, too few people to work 'em. And right now? I need some sleep."

"Why don't Ray and I make the casino trip?" said Osborne.

"Have to be back by three for me to pick up Gina," said Ray.

"That should work," said Osborne.

"Depends how long we take with the Nehlsons," said Lew. At the surprise on Osborne's face, she said, "I'm planning on you being there, Doc. The usual routine: I talk, you watch. Vice versa. On second thought . . ." She tipped her head as she gave Ray a long look.

"I'd like you there, too, Ray. You and Doc both knew Peg over the years. Think you can handle that, Ray?"

"I think so. Actually, I would like to be there. I'd like to ask the family if I might say a few words at Peg's funeral."

"Why don't you plan to do that after the meeting. I'd like to see how things go first."

"Sure."

"Okay—we've got a plan. See you two in the morning."

"Wait. One more thing, Chief. I've been thinking about Robbie's comment on that gas tank," said Ray. "Why don't I get Gina settled—"

"I'll have Marlene find space for her in the department, Ray. She'll need high-speed Internet access, and I doubt her cottage will have that."

"Okay," said Ray, "so I'll get Gina set up and then I'll take a drive around. Ever since you said Pat's old lady told you they stopped for gas and one last drink on their way home from karaoke, I've been thinking about where they might have gone. A couple places have come to mind."

"Fine with me," said Lew, standing up. "Now I'm out of here. I am dead tired."

• • •

"Lewellyn, fatigue becomes you," said Osborne, ruffling her hair as he walked her to the car. She gave him a rueful smile as she opened the car door.

"I can't afford to be so tired—I'm afraid I'll miss something, Doc."

"I miss this," he said, pulling her toward him.

"Me, too." She folded herself into his embrace, tired and warm.

"When this is over, Lew, maybe we can spend some time together? It's been over a week now . . ."

She gave him a quick, light kiss that held all the sweetness of the raspberries. "You know I love to fish a full moon."

"Two nights from now?"

"Two nights from now," she said, "plan on it. I'll loan you a float tube and we'll go up to Sylvania."

After Ray left, Osborne checked his answering machine. He had two messages. The first was from his elder daughter, Mallory: "Dad, I need a break. Turned in a paper on marketing cosmetic dentistry today and could really use some time away from the computer. Hope you don't mind if I drive up for the weekend—take you to fish fry. Call if this is a problem."

He checked his watch: too late to call. It wasn't that he didn't want to see her. The question was: Would she understand why he couldn't spend much time with her? Over the last two years they had been fumbling toward a better relationship, but Mallory had yet to give up one bad habit she had inherited from her mother: She was too quick to have her feelings hurt.

And why was it that she and Gina Palmer had to be here the same weekend? Two women who were way too interested in a man who, should they succeed in netting him, they would have to support. Well, he'd leave that juggling act to Ray. They were all adults. Let those three figure it out.

The second message was from his oldest grandchild, eleven-year-old Beth: "Gramps, I got an e-mail today from some lady who's hunting you. Mom told me to tell you to stop by the house in the morning so we can show you the e-mail. The lady wants your phone number but Mom said I can't give it to her until you say it's okay."

Hunting me? Osborne didn't like the sound of that.

Twenty minutes later, Mike asleep beside his bed, the window above his pillow wide open, Osborne lay listening to the strains of country music drifting over the water. Likely Shania Twain, he thought. He had set his clock to wake up an hour earlier than usual—so much to be done in the morning.

He was happy thinking ahead: A full day is always a good day.

fifteen

Every man has a fish in his life that haunts him.

—Negley Farson

Erin's house was quiet. Standing on the front porch of the old Victorian, Osborne peered through the screen door into the living room. He hesitated knocking in case the kids were still asleep. His son-in-law, he knew, would be long gone. Mark prided himself on being at his desk in the Loon Lake District Attorney's Office by seven at the latest.

Erin might be up. Even though she was working her way toward a law degree, this summer she had elected to take just one course. That plus three lively children, a new puppy, and volunteering at the library made for a day that had to start early.

Osborne rapped lightly on the door frame then slowly pulled open the screen door, only to have a four-month-old black Lab come bounding at him through the living room—followed by a loud, "No, Bruno, no!"

Erin appeared in the doorway that led to the kitchen, coffee mug in hand. "Careful, Dad! Don't let him out," she said. "C'mon in—got a full pot here for you."

Osborne walked through the long, high-ceilinged living room. The windows had been pushed up as high as they would go, and morning breezes nudged at the ivory lace curtains. The house felt full of fresh air and sun—just like Erin. She was busy buttering toast, and at her elbow was a bowl of eggs ready for scrambling.

As he entered the kitchen, she set the toast aside, handed him a steaming mug of hot coffee, and motioned toward the kitchen table. He loved seeing her early in the morning—her long blond hair pulled back in a single braid, her face scrubbed and free of makeup. This particular day she was in running shorts and a tank top that emphasized her slim figure.

"You run already?" said Osborne, pulling out a chair.

"Four miles before Mark left for the office. Too hot later—supposed to hit ninety today." She sat down with her own mug of coffee, took a deep sip and said, "Ah-h-h, a moment of peace before the monsters awake."

Erin slapped the table with her free hand, startling Osborne, who spilled a few drops of his coffee. "Dad, I was so upset to hear about Peg Garmin. I woke up during the night thinking about it. What I want to know is if she found her son before she died? I mean—this is so sad. *So* unfair."

"What are you talking about?" said Osborne, reaching for a paper napkin to wipe up the spill. "What son? I didn't know she and Frank had any children."

"Not from her marriage. She had a child out of wedlock and decided to try to find him a couple months ago. She came to the library looking for books on how to find people who were adopted. I told her she would have better luck using the Internet.

"Since she wasn't familiar with computers, I helped her get started. It wasn't too difficult—she had the name of the hospital, the date of birth, and she remembered the Catholic girls home where she stayed during her pregnancy. She was able to reach the adoption agency not long after that."

As their mother spoke, Osborne's three grandchildren started to wander into the kitchen, still in their pajamas and sleepy-eyed: Cody, nearly four; Mason, eight; and Beth, on the brink of puberty.

The eleven-year-old snuggled into Osborne, laying one arm across his shoulders. She was about to whisper in his ear when her mother said, "Beth, you can show Gramps the e-mail in a few minutes. We're having a grown-up conversation right now. You three—out!" She pointed to the door behind her. "Take Bruno to the backyard. I'll call when your eggs are ready."

As the screen door slammed behind the kids, Erin said, "When it comes to Peg—you never know what's going to come up, so I'd rather they not be around."

"That's okay with me," said Osborne. "The details are too grim for kids, believe me."

"Mark said you were the deputy coroner at the scene yesterday."

Osborne nodded. "I've never seen anything like it. He probably told you—it's a triple homicide."

"Yeah, on top of everything else going on around here," said Erin. "Are you helping out?"

"Ray and I both are—have a busy day ahead." He checked his watch. It was only seven-thirty. He didn't think it polite to call Harold Westbrook before eight.

"We're all meeting in Lew's office with Peg's sister and her husband at nine. But let's go back to what you were saying about Peg putting a child up for adoption. I find that very interesting. You're the first person to mention it." He reached into his shirt pocket for his notebook and the case with his reading glasses.

"She told me she didn't want anyone to know until she was sure she could find him. Dad, it was early last week that she stopped in just to tell me that the adoption agency was being very cooperative because the young man—I think he would be in his early thirties—had been in touch with them, too. He was looking for her. She was so excited. That's why it's such a shame that—"

"You don't happen to know what his name is?"

"No. That never came up in our conversations. But I have the information on the adoption agency in my files at the library. I kept a hard copy in case Peg lost hers. If you want, I can get that for you later this morning."

"Anything else that you think might help?"

"Well . . . she was considering a lawsuit over some plastic surgery that went wrong. Do you know about that?"

"A little," said Osborne. "I know she was seeking a second opinion."

"Right. She hadn't been able to get the surgeon who did the work to agree to repair the damage. So the other thing I helped her with was an Internet search to get the names of a few professionals she might approach for a second opinion."

"So *that's* how she found Gerry Rasmussen!"

"Yes." It was Erin's turn to be surprised. "Do you know him?"

"We've met through dental circles. When Lew and I were searching Peg's place last night, we found a letter from his office. I spoke with him this morning. What I've been wondering ever since is—what possessed her to go to an oral surgeon? Why not get an opinion from another *plastic* surgeon?"

"Ah, Dad. Good question. And I'm the one responsible for putting her in touch with Dr. Rasmussen. More coffee?"

"Please."

"When Peg told me what her problem was, we did a Google search on medical malpractice. One of the articles we found recommended that anyone with questions regarding surgeries involving the head and the neck should consider an opinion from a maxillofacial surgeon in addition to a plastic surgeon. So we went to the Wisconsin Dental Society's Web site and that's how we found Dr. Rasmussen."

As she spoke, Osborne recalled the conversation he had had earlier that morning with Dr. Gerald Rasmussen, D.D.S. One of the benefits of retaining his membership in the Wisconsin Dental Society was the annual roster with office and home numbers. After placing an initial call to Rasmussen's office and hearing a voice message encouraging anyone with an emergency to try the home number—he did.

It was six-thirty when Osborne reached the oral surgeon at his breakfast table. After explaining the reason for his call, Gerry was eager to talk. More than eager: fired up. It seems that Peg Garmin's request for a second opinion from a maxillofacial surgeon had ignited quite a debate between the two state societies representing plastic surgeons and dentists. And Rasmussen was plenty angry.

"Those of us who are board certified in O.M.S. practice are sick and tired of what we're seeing in the field of cosmetic surgery. I'll tell you, Paul, the damage some of these fools are doing . . ." said Gerry, so apoplectic he was choking.

"It is audacious—just incredible some of the mistakes I've seen. One idiot stopped just short of setting a lower jaw *outside* the mouth."

"Now, Gerry, aren't you exaggerating just a bit?" said Osborne.

"I wish I were. I tell you, Paul, there is so much money to be made in cosmetic surgery that you get these commodes who have an M.D. degree and minimal surgical training who hang out a shingle for plastic surgery. They aren't board certified, but hell, that doesn't stop them.

"That Forsythe fellow is a perfect example. I don't know how the Garmin woman found him, but boy oh boy, did he do a lousy job on her face. And I will bet you anything she isn't the first. But that's for her lawyer to determine.

"I find the whole thing disgusting, Paul," said Rasmussen, speaking with such intensity that Osborne stopped trying to interrupt with questions. It was hopeless to do anything but listen as he ranted, "I am sick and tired of the attitude I'm getting from some of these plastic surgeon types. You want to know why I am happy to offer my services as an expert witness? That's why: the arrogance of some of these guys.

"Look at the reality for a minute. Someone is in a horrible accident, half their face torn off, and who's called? Me. I go in, I reattach every muscle and piece of skin and bone. I do all the follow-up surgeries to be sure everything is perfect. Right? Meanwhile, I'm paid half what a plastic surgeon is for the same work.

"But if someone comes in with a bad nose from birth or from some previous surgery—I'm not allowed to touch it. All of a sudden all I am is the guy who can pull teeth and treat a lower jaw fracture.

"Well, I've had it," said Rasmussen, "and I'm pushing to expand the definition of dentistry in this state. For heaven's sake, professionals like me have four to seven years of post-dental-school surgical hospital residency. *We* are the head and neck experts."

Rasmussen paused to take a breath and Osborne jumped in: "Gerry, do you mind going back to Peg Garmin for a minute? What went wrong exactly?"

"Sloppy technique. That's what went wrong. And I've heard other complaints along the same line. Same guy, too.

"See, Forsythe is big on injections. When you do that, you work with a sharp needle, which means technique is crucial. In the Garmin case, he was giving her an injection in the face, the needle slipped, and an artery was pierced. The fat that was being injected blocked some capillaries, shut off the blood flow, and caused the soft tissue on one side of the nose to die and slough off.

"Poor woman. She looked like half her nose had caved in."

"Okay, Beth, you can come in and show your grandfather that e-mail now," said Erin, opening the back door. The youngster came flying up the steps and into the kitchen. She grabbed Osborne's hand and pulled him back to the family room. Giving him a big smile, she settled herself on the stool in front of the family's computer, hit a key, and waited.

The e-mail was from a woman whose name Osborne had not heard in nearly fifty years: Beebo McElhenny Rowland, sister of his best friend at the age of fourteen. The e-mail was addressed to Erin, who used "Osborne" as her middle name.

"I think you may be related to Paul Osborne, the dentist," wrote the stranger. "I've been able to locate your e-mail address but can find nothing for Paul. If you know him or if you are related, would you please pass on this message for me?

"Years ago, he was the best friend of my older brother, Bud. They were roommates at boarding school, Campion. Paul spent several vacations with our family. The last I heard about Paul was that he had married and opened a dental practice in northern Wisconsin.

"My husband passed away two years ago and I've been having a wonderful time reconnecting with old friends. Please let Paul and his wife have my phone number—if I do indeed have the correct Paul Osborne. Tell him I apologize for hunting him down but I have fond memories of him from those days . . ." The e-mail carried the name "Beebo Rowland."

Beth looked up expectantly. Erin, standing quietly behind him, gave Osborne a teasing poke in the ribs. "Okay, Dad, what do you want Beth to say? How should we respond?"

"I—I don't know," said Osborne. The last time he saw Beebo, she wasn't much older than Beth. Thirteen at the most. But thirteen going on thirty. She was the first girl he ever kissed. The first girl he had enjoyed thinking about in ways that made for embarrassing moments in the confessional. For over a year, Beebo had been his first and last thought of the day.

"Well . . . what do *you* think?" he turned to Erin.

"Go for it, Dad." She grinned.

"Gee . . . I don't know," said Osborne. "I've got my hands full helping Lew right now—"

"Dad," said Erin, "a phone call? You can manage a *phone* call, for heaven's sake. She sounds sweet. And, Dad, you never know. Besides, she thinks you're married. So what's wrong with catching up with an old friend?"

sixteen

*It is just possible that nice guys don't catch the most fish.
But they find more pleasure in those they do get.*

—Roderick Haig-Brown

Osborne hurried up the paved walk leading to the front
door of the elegant red brick home. Before he could knock,
Harold Westbrook opened the door.

"Paul, come in," he said. "I heard about Peg on the
news last night. But I didn't know whom to call. I tried the
police—the woman on the switchboard wouldn't tell me a
thing. The sheriff's office knew nothing.

"Can you tell me how it happened? She was—" Press-
ing his fingers to his eyes, he choked up and motioned for
Osborne to follow him through the spacious foyer, past the
formal living room to a den off the kitchen.

Half the room was neatly outfitted with equipment and
supplies for tying trout flies. The other half held an old
roll-top oak desk, a high-backed chair with an ottoman—
both facing a wall-mounted flat-screen television—and a
small leather sofa guarded by an impressive elk mount.
Two mallards in flight haunted the wall above the desk.

"How much time did you say you had? Need coffee?"
Harold's hands shook as he spoke and his eyes were blood-
shot.

"No coffee, thank you. Chief Ferris and I are meeting with the family at nine—Peg's sister and her husband. So we've got some time, Harold."

Osborne checked his watch. It was eight-fifteen. After reaching the widower by phone a few minutes earlier, he had decided it would be just as fast to walk from Erin's house. The Westbrook residence was only two and a half blocks away and Harold sounded anxious to see him.

The retired physician was tall and large-boned with wide shoulders. He looked strong, which was typical of other thoracic surgeons that Osborne had known, and he walked with the stride of a man much younger than eighty. This morning, however, he looked his age: his shock of white hair whiter than ever against the flush of his face. It was obvious he had been crying.

Harold waved Osborne toward the sofa, then seated himself in the armchair.

"I missed the news," said Osborne. "What did they say?"

"They interviewed the father of one of the other women," said Harold.

"That would have been Ralph Federer, Donna's father," said Osborne. He wondered if Lew knew that Channel 12 had scored after all.

"He said there were three victims in the car and foul play was suspected. Not much more than that. But when he mentioned the names of the women and I heard Peg's . . ." The old man's reddened eyes searched Osborne's. "She was a dear, dear friend . . . what more you can tell me?" His voice cracked with sadness.

"I'll tell you what we know so far," said Osborne and took him briefly through the details. "Now, none of this is public knowledge, Harold."

"I'll respect that, Paul. And I will assume you will keep

some of what I tell you in confidence unless it is material to Chief Ferris's investigation? I have been an expert witness myself enough times to know complete privacy may not be possible, but I want to do whatever I can to help find who did this."

Sitting back in the armchair with his legs crossed and his hands resting in his lap, the man was somber and poised. Osborne regretted he had never taken the time to get to know him better.

"My relationship with Peg . . ." Harold's voice trailed off. Osborne shifted in his chair, uncertain what to say. How do you ask a man about his mistress? Worse, how do you ask him about the other men in her life? Harold saved him the effort on the first question.

"I started seeing her after my wife died four years ago. That's never been a secret in this town. And yes, it started as a physical relationship, which I very much wanted at the time. Was willing to pay for." He gave a grim laugh.

"My wife and I were of a generation that did not believe in divorce. I think I bored my wife. I *know* I bored my wife."

"You mean she wasn't into tying trout flies?"

Harold looked at him in amazement for a split second, then burst into a loud guffaw. "Tying trout flies was the least of what she wasn't interested in." He paused, reflecting, then said, "You know that old quote—'Some men lead lives of quiet desperation . . .'"

Osborne nodded in understanding. Complete and total understanding.

"So early on in my marriage I became familiar with women like Peg. Or so I thought at first—that Peg was like all the others.

"The thing is . . ." Harold hesitated as if he was still trying to figure something out. "She was different . . ." He paused. "I'm not sure how to put this . . . she had an ethe-real quality to her. She didn't have that edge. We got along. From the very first, we got along. It was nice. *She* was nice.

"Before I knew it, we had moved from having sex to just enjoying our conversations. That's the best way I can put it. And that doesn't happen that often—with anyone. You know?" Harold gave a slight smile as he spoke.

"I know exactly what you mean," said Osborne, think-ing of his hours driving, in the trout stream, or just being with Lew.

"You may find this difficult to believe"—Harold dropped his head, then raised it as if challenging Osborne's opinion—"but under that gloss of makeup and dyed hair was a delicate human being. Delicate . . . thoughtful . . . kind. One of those rare people who knows how to be a friend. A good, good friend. She seemed to enjoy listening to me for hours—loved to hear about my work, loved hearing how my fishing went, my golf game."

He uncrossed his legs, shifted in his chair, then said, "We had a routine, you see. On Sunday evenings, she came for cocktails and I cooked dinner. Mondays, Tuesdays, and Thursdays, she came for cocktails—and *she* cooked din-ner. Gosh, how those evenings flew by. Peg was a good conversationalist. She read a lot, she was well educated. She was just . . ." His voice trailed off. Osborne waited.

"So some nights she slept here, some nights she went home. Maybe we drank a little too much—but we enjoyed one another. As companions. You know, Paul, at my age it doesn't hurt to have a woman in your bed simply to hold you."

"Harold," said Osborne, "would it help if I told you that you're not the only person I know who thought the world of Peg Garmin? Who loved her?"

"Really? I'm glad to hear that. I wasn't sure anyone else knew her as she really was."

"You used the word 'delicate,'" said Osborne.

"Yes. I came to think of her as my delicate angel with the damaged wings." Harold nodded, affirming the fact. "Very damaged."

"And what made you think that?"

"Well, these conversations we were having—after a time, she began to open up to me about her life. I wanted to hear, you know." Harold's expression darkened. "Paul, how familiar are you with her background? Before her marriage to that Frank fellow?"

"We don't know much," said Osborne. "Going through her belongings last night, Chief Ferris and I found some photos—"

"I'm talking about her childhood." Harold slammed his fist on the arm of his chair. "She was adopted and abused. Molested by the father of the family that adopted her, which I guarantee was the root cause of all the other problems."

"She told you that?"

"The story eked out over time. I don't know what hurt her more—the actual abuse or that no one in that family believed her. She was trapped. I know she ran away as soon as she could and spent most of her adult life estranged from those people.

"In my opinion that's why she slipped into prostitution. Why else would that happen? The woman came from wealth. You do know she was one of the Chicago Garmins, right?"

"Yes," said Osborne. "But not many people in Loon Lake have made that connection."

"She didn't want them to. She didn't want to have anything to do with those people. But six months ago they came barging back into her life."

"What do you mean?"

"Ah," said Harold, "you don't know about this? Good. Then I do have something to contribute. One day Peg gets a letter in the mail from the old lady: the classic deathbed plea for forgiveness.

"Old Mrs. Garmin, on the brink of dying from cancer, decided to admit to knowing all along that her husband had abused Peg. Then she tried to make it right with money." Harold snorted. "Isn't it always about money?" He shook his head in disgust. "As if money could make a little girl whole again."

"How much are you talking about, Harold?" said Osborne.

"Forty-eight million dollars."

Osborne gave a low whistle.

"Peg didn't want the money. She didn't need it. I have no heirs. Two years ago, I set her up with a trust. At first she was going to refuse the Garmin money, but I convinced her otherwise. Maybe I was wrong—but her plan was to give it away anyway."

"To her son, perhaps?"

"What?" Harold stared at Osborne.

"My daughter, Erin, works at the library and has been helping her search for the child she gave up for adoption years ago."

Harold sat with his mouth open. "So *that's* what she was up to. She was so tickled over some 'surprise' that she kept talking about. She wouldn't tell me the details. She said it was a secret and I would know soon enough.

"Paul, that is what I have been wondering since I heard the news last night: Peg's secret. Is that what got her killed?"

seventeen

If you wish to be happy for an hour, get intoxicated.
If you wish to be happy for three days, get married.
If you wish to be happy for eight days, kill your pig
*   and eat it.*
If you wish to be happy forever, learn to fish.

—Chinese proverb

"What about the other men?" said Osborne, slipping in the tough question as he got to his feet. "Was there anyone she was seeing who—"

"No other men," said Harold, his voice firm. "That was our agreement when I set up the trust."

"So she hasn't . . . didn't . . . for two years?"

"Correct. No need to. She enriched my life and I decided I wanted to take care of her."

"Well . . . that's kind of a surprise. I think we all thought—"

"Paul, I don't give a damn what people around here thought. I made sure she didn't need money and then one day, ironically, she turns out to be the heiress to a fortune. I like to think that being with me made her feel good enough about herself that she didn't need other men. Like a lot of women, she was never happy with how she looked—no matter what I said."

"So you know about that—the problem with her face," said Osborne as he neared the front door. "It appears she was filing a lawsuit?"

"Damn right she was. I helped her with that even though I didn't think she looked all that bad. But the damage to her nose should not have happened. The plastic surgeon—Ed Forsyth is his name. What a dumyak. I've got all the information if you need it. His offices are in Milwaukee. The guy did a lousy, sloppy job. On top of which he refused to repair the damage without charge. He wanted a fee as if it were an entire new surgery. A scam—that's all it was. An absolute scam."

Harold paused, resting his hand on the front doorknob. "You know—now that you mention it, Peg's first appointment with the lawyer was scheduled for next week. Good man, too. I put her in touch with Rick Knudson—one of the best when it comes to medical malpractice. And fair.

"This was not about money, by the way. Peg did not need any more money. Quite the contrary—she was willing to spend whatever she had to—to bring the guy down. She was convinced that Forsyth was taking advantage of other women she knew. She wanted him stopped."

"Harold, you've been very helpful. I'm sure that either myself or Chief Ferris will be calling you back," said Osborne. "Sorry to rush out like this." He stepped onto the walk then turned. "One last question. You're aware that Peg's late husband had quite the checkered past. Do you know if anyone from those days might have contacted her recently? Bothered her? Any threats of any kind?"

"No, not that she mentioned. Paul, I do think she would have told me if she was feeling threatened by anyone. No—the only matters disturbing her over the last few months had to do with that botched surgery and the evil memories behind the Garmin money."

Osborne started down the walk. "Paul," said Harold from his doorway, "I've never met Peg's family. Would you let them know that I would like to say a few words at the memorial service? I would very much like to do that."

"I tell you that fish was so huge, my rig felt like a chopstick with dental floss." Ray had draped himself over the glass panel fronting the switchboard in the entrance to the police station. "If that line had snapped, I'd still be circling the globe."

Marlene on the switchboard chortled. Her wide, freckled face under an explosion of red-brown curls beamed up at Ray, who was quite dapper in crisp khakis and a white T-shirt. She glanced over as Osborne walked toward them.

"Good morning, Doc. Ray's been regaling me with his latest whopper. The Nehlsons haven't arrived yet and Chief Ferris is on the phone."

"He's not pulling your leg, Marlene. I'll bet that was a fifty-inch muskie he had on the line last night," said Osborne, relieved to see that Ray was in good form.

"Oh, Chief's off the phone," said Marlene. "I know she wants you both back in her office."

"She ready to commensurate?" said Ray.

"I think you mean commiserate," said Osborne.

"Yeah, commensurate," said Ray. He gave Marlene a wink. "Bye now, pay later."

Walking down the hallway behind his neighbor, Osborne noticed Ray's shirt had an inscription on the back: SO MANY MOSQUITOES—SO FEW RECIPES.

He should have known. But what the heck, at least the guy was his old self. As they entered her office, Lew set some paperwork to one side of her desk and stood up.

The long, high-ceilinged room, which was in the old section of the courthouse, was airy and full of light. Pots of spring green asparagus fern, set along the window ledges, cascaded to the floor. From behind the ferns, the open windows let in a soft buzz of employees chatting over coffee at picnic tables set out on the lawn.

Lew looked rested. "Good morning, you two," she said, reaching for her empty coffee mug. "Grab a cup of coffee and take a seat around the table there. I expect the Nehlsons any minute—Joan and Parker are their names. They were to stop by the morgue and complete the paperwork with Pecore."

"So what was his excuse for never showing up yesterday?" said Osborne.

"Alleges the wind blew your note from his windshield. I asked him if that was the same wind that blew my messages off his answering machine."

"And?"

Before she could answer, Ray, who was standing before the front windows, hands in his pockets as he gazed at the activity on the courthouse lawn, said, "Whoa, check that out."

All three watched as a black Lincoln Navigator backed into a parking spot. Even from a distance the limited edition's brass accents gleamed gold in the morning sun.

"That's moola," said Ray.

Now it was Lew's turn to read the back of Ray's shirt. She caught Osborne's eye—she was as relieved as he was.

As they waited for the couple, Lew indicated to both to sit down. They would have at least five minutes, which was what it would take for the Nehlsons to walk up the long sidewalk to the courthouse, past the windows—which included Lew's—along the front of the building and around to the back, where the entrance to the police department was located.

Osborne gave Lew and Ray a quick rundown on what

he had learned from Harold. Ray's eyebrows hit the ceiling when he mentioned the inheritance.

"She never mentioned a word of that," he said.

"Ray had a good morning, too," said Lew.

"Yep," said Ray. "Checked out three bars with gas pumps this morning and found the one where the girls had their last drink. The bartender who served them is working tonight. Doc, I thought you and me and Chief Ferris and Gina might catch a fish fry and stop in there later this evening."

"Better include Mallory," said Osborne. "She left a message she's driving up today."

"Oh," said Ray, wrinkling his brow.

eighteen

They may the better fish in the water when it is troubled.

—Richard Grafton

Joan Nehlson strode into the room as if taking it hostage. Osborne's first impression was of a black monolith coming at him. Early in his youth, before figuring the financial consequences, he had entertained pursuing sculpture as a career. Ever since then he'd had a habit of seeing strangers as volumes: squares, spheres, rhomboids.

This was one long, tall oblong under a hard-edged cap of acid yellow hair. The teeth, Chiclets-styled in two too-perfect rows, were oblong under a lengthy rectangle of nose. As if to argue the reality of her shape, the woman had cinched a long-sleeved black shirt over black slacks with a wide belt. But not even the aggressive cinching of the belt could hide the fact that the waistline was long gone.

The Chiclet teeth flashed at Osborne as she thrust out her hand. "Good morning, Chief Ferris, sorry we're a little late."

The voice was unreasonably loud for the square footage of the room. Though her face was smooth and well made-up, an impression of horsiness prevailed. Osborne had a sudden and unkind thought: This was one of those women who had inherited too many of their father's physical attributes.

"Dr. Paul Osborne, just a deputy on the case," said Osborne, beckoning toward Lew, who was standing behind her desk. "This is Loon Lake's Chief of Police, Lewellyn Ferris." Osborne made the decision to keep his voice low and professional—the tone he used when advising a patient who professed to know more about dentistry than the dentist.

"Oh?" said Joan, leaning back on a pair of low heels as she turned, "Well, isn't that interesting. My husband didn't tell me he spoke with a woman." Her tone implied the mistake must be Loon Lake's for choosing a female to head up their law enforcement team.

From the side, Osborne could see one similarity between Joan and her adopted sister, Peg, and that was across the cheekbones. Peg had had wide, rounded cheekbones, always slightly flushed, that gave her face a heart shape. If you looked closely and imagined this woman fifty pounds lighter, you might find similar cheekbones. Not surprising, as couples adopting children often seek out youngsters with some physical resemblance to themselves. In a bad light, you might guess the two women to be sisters by birth.

Another figure had slipped into the room behind Joan. Osborne assumed it was her husband. He was slightly shorter than his wife and of medium build. His face under wisps of grey hair was quite round and so pale he reminded Osborne of one of Ray's unbaked piecrusts. He stood just inside the doorway, not anxious to interrupt.

"Oh—and this is my husband, Parker," said Joan, with a backward wave of her hand. She caught sight of the coffeepot and said, "Oh! Say—could I have a cup?" Before anyone could answer, she was up and pouring herself a cup. She looked around. "Do you have a straw?"

"For your coffee?" said Lew.

"Of course. So it won't stain my teeth."

Lew threw a look at Osborne, who shrugged. This was a new one to him.

"We know that up until five years ago, your sister and her husband ran Deer Haven," said Lew, opening the discussion. "Nice resort on good muskie water. Your sister was known to many people here in Loon Lake—"

"I'll bet she was," said Joan with a snort. "Don't waste time being polite, I know what my sister was—she was a whore. And that is very likely what got her killed."

"Your sister was kind and gracious and many people liked her," said Ray, his voice rising ever so slightly.

"Really." Joan turned toward Ray, disbelief ringing in her words. "You'll have a tough time convincing me of that. Or anyone else in the family—our late parents in particular. How about you, Parker? Wouldn't you agree?"

Before her husband could answer, she said, "It's a fact. You take a chance when you adopt. My parents got a wacko. No matter how hard they tried—that girl was bad from the start. *Born bad.*"

And with that, Joan launched into an authoritative review of Peg's history: teenage promiscuity, running away—years of drugs and prostitution. She punctuated her words with angry jabs of well-manicured hands.

"Now throw in Frank." She sniffed and threw her hands up in the air. "She married a corrupt cop, for God's sake."

"Yes," said Lew, who sat with her elbows on the desk, chin resting on her folded hands. In sharp contrast to the sister's histrionics, Lew was calm and deft in her response. "We know all about Frank. The question I have is whether you think someone from his past might have had a grudge against Peg? Or some other motive for killing her?"

"That's where I was hoping you would start," said Joan. "After Frank died, all hell broke loose. You tell them, Parker. How many times did we have to send her money? Had to make bail even. She got herself beat up a few years back." Parker nodded in silence.

"Any one person specifically?"

"How about recent . . . clients?" said Joan.

"Well, we have reason to believe that recently she had been seeing only one person and that was a retired physician here. A straightforward relationship—the kind you would expect to find between any two consenting adults. No funny business."

"That's a surprise. But I wouldn't know, to tell you the truth. I kept my distance from Peg. Didn't need any of *that* in our lives. You know, we live in Kenilworth, which is one of Chicago's nicer suburbs. Our family is well known in the community—we don't seek out bad press."

"So even though you have a summer home an hour from here, you had no contact with Peg?" said Ray, his voice measured. "But in fact, you sent her money. Isn't that what you just said?"

"We sent money a few times, but that was a while ago. Parker drove up to Green Bay when she was hospitalized after the beating. I haven't *spoken* to her in months. We had minimal contact, is how I would put it. Minimal."

"When was it that you made bail for her?" said Lew, looking at Parker.

"Four years ago," said Joan.

"She was asking your husband," said Ray, his voice gentle.

"I know that," said Joan, squinting to stare at him. "And just who the hell are *you*?"

"I'm sorry. I thought he was introduced to you earlier," said Lew before Ray could answer. "Ray Pradt is one of two deputies working the case with me. He and Dr. Osborne are helping out. We have three victims and a great deal of work that has to be done. Dr. Osborne was your sister's dentist, by the way. So he's known her since she moved up here."

Joan rolled her eyes at her husband, a look that implied she was talking with the Three Stooges.

"Now . . . I take it you were *not* adopted," said Lew, changing the subject.

The Chiclet smile turned smug as Joan said, "Heavens, no. I was conceived two years after they got Peg."

"More siblings?"

"Just the two of us."

"Well then, I imagine you must have been their favorite," said Lew in a gentle tone.

Again the smugness. "I was better behaved. I didn't cause them grief."

"Is that why she inherited forty-eight million dollars?" said Ray.

"You know," said Joan, pushing her chair back, "I don't like your attitude."

"We learned about the inheritance just this morning," said Lew.

"Before you go any further down that road, let me assure you that my mother's will is being challenged in court. She was suffering from dementia when she decided to leave Peg . . . some of the estate."

"I see," said Lew. "We assumed it might have been an act of remorse relative to the abuse that your sister suffered as a child."

"All right," said Joan, who was sitting with her legs crossed. Now her lips tightened as her right foot pumped up and down. She shook an index finger at Lew. "I want to know who you've been talking to because that is an old, old story and an absolute lie. Peg made it up—her way of getting attention. It was all in her head."

"Do you mind if I ask how old you were at the time the abuse was alleged to have occurred?" said Lew in a brisk tone.

"Five. But I heard the story many times over the years. My parents were devastated. No one ever believed it. No one." She looked down at the floor as she spoke, as if avoiding something distasteful.

"I apologize for questions like these," said Lew, "but you can understand when three people are murdered. All three families have to deal with some disturbing issues. Has anyone notified Peg's son of her death? The one she gave up for adoption? We think they may have been in touch. Just a courtesy, you know."

Joan did a double take. Her voice dropped to a normal level for the first time as she said, "Now you *are* kidding. There is no child. Peg managed to get herself pregnant without benefit of a ring but the baby was born dead. Right, Parker?"

Parker offered his hands in a gesture of supplication and shrugged. He looked so confused that Osborne wondered if he knew where he was and what he was doing.

"Okay"—Lew checked her watch—"just a few more questions. Doc and Ray have an appointment up north and I have some other matters to attend to before noon."

"Does the name 'Edward Forsyth' mean anything to you?"

"Of course. He's our neighbor on the lake. He owns the property next to ours. We're good friends."

"Did you know your sister was filing a lawsuit against him?"

"No!" said Joan, surprise on her face. "She told me she was pleased with the work he did."

"Oh, I thought you had minimal contact with your sister," said Lew.

"Giving her a recommendation of a plastic surgeon over a year ago is pretty minimal in my estimation. You know," said Joan with a shake of her head, "nothing about my sister was real. She'd had her breasts done, maybe a tummy tuck—and she called me because she wanted a face-lift. Ed is terrific. That's how she found him. I can't believe she was filing a lawsuit. Poor Ed."

"We'll be checking into that," said Lew. "You wouldn't happen to know if Dr. Forsyth is in the area—coming up for the weekend maybe?"

"Yes, I do. We've invited him for dinner tomorrow evening," said Joan.

"Do you have a phone number for Dr. Forsyth's lake residence?" asked Lew.

"Somewhere in here," said Joan, rummaging through her purse.

"Before you folks leave," said Osborne as they waited, "I wanted to mention that Dr. Harold Westbrook, Peg's good friend these past few years, would like to say a few words at her memorial service."

"Oh, there'll be no service," said Joan. "Once those lab people are finished, I'll have her cremated and Parker and I will dispose of the remains. Given the family history . . . you know."

There was a long silence in the room.

"Are you finished with us?" said Joan. "You have our number if you have more questions."

"Yes, thank you," said Lew and showed them to the door. "This has been very helpful."

When they had reached the end of the hall, Ray said,

"The husband never said a word. You think she put anesthesia in his coffee?"

"Or he's hung-over," said Osborne.

"Or just following orders," said Lew. "Easy to tell who wears the pants in that family."

"That woman is as hard as Peg was soft," said Ray.

The Nehlsons never looked to their right as they walked past the windows along the front of the courthouse. Inside, Lew was gathering up her notes as Ray and Osborne sauntered toward the door, hanging back to walk out with her.

"Why did you say that about Peg's child?" The masculine voice floated through the open windows.

"I dunno. Just popped out. They can't trace that kid. We don't even know what happened to him."

"I would like to know," said Parker.

"Oh, for chrissakes," said his wife, contempt ringing in her voice.

They turned left down the sidewalk toward their car.

nineteen

The end of fishing is not angling, but catching.

—Thomas Fuller

Knowing that Ray would have to leave in time to meet Gina's plane, they decided to take two cars. It was a forty-minute drive northwest, a drive that Osborne always enjoyed as the pines grew taller, closing in on the road to lend the region the look of virgin timber. It wasn't—but it was landscaped, planted, and patrolled to appear so.

This was expensive lake country with commercial development limited so as not to mar the views of the McMansions under construction at the end of lanes, well hidden from public view. Only the signs fronting the private roads—white arrows with names painted black and stacked one on top of the other, often as many as twenty or thirty—hinted at the number of summer residents lining the lakes.

Osborne tended to drive past the signs without paying attention, but today he kept an eye out. Sure enough, just past the cranberry bogs Dick Wallace had recently sold to Ocean Spray, he spotted what he was looking for—two signs, one nailed above the other: FORSYTH and NEHLSON. The signs were freshly painted and the only two marking the road.

•　•　•

Twenty minutes later, Osborne pulled alongside Ray's pickup in the packed parking lot of the Moonlight Casino. Entering the casino, Osborne wasn't sure if it was the noise, the lights, or the guy with the mullet who pushed him going through the door that got to him first. Or maybe it was the guy's girlfriend who seemed to think her aggressive display of cleavage would neutralize an urgent need for orthodontia. Everywhere he looked things were throbbing: ropes of neon, panels on slot machines, even the air. Worst of all—outdoors was a gorgeous summer day and the place was packed. Just packed.

Ray was on his tiptoes, peering over the banks of slot machines and clouds of cigarette smoke that fogged in the blackjack tables. "Hold on, Doc. Looking for a guy I know . . ."

"Is there a guy anywhere you don't know?" said Osborne. Driving out of Loon Lake forty minutes earlier, Osborne in his car following Ray in his battered pickup, he had watched his neighbor wave to every person he saw. This included oncoming traffic, kids on their bikes, mothers pushing strollers, runners. And they all smiled as they waved back.

Ray touched Osborne's shoulder lightly and tipped his head. "See the guy in the corner, Doc? That's who we want—Gib Salisbury. He's been running the poker room for the last couple years. He's a client of mine, but I never charge him."

"You never charge him?" said Osborne.

"Referrals," said Ray as he guided the two of them back toward the bar near the poker room. "When some guys get a run of luck and the casino needs to break their momentum, there's nothing like a little muskie fishing. And he's sent me some big rollers. Nice tips."

"I guess that explains the bag of ice and bluegills in your right hand?"

"You betcha. This man *l-o-v-ves* a fresh bluegill."

"Gentlemen, you aren't asking the right questions," drawled Gib Salisbury. The elderly black man sat casually at the bar, nursing a Coke on the rocks. After fifteen minutes of small talk, Osborne finally had a chance to raise the subject of Donna and her training to be a poker dealer.

He had waited patiently for a sign from Ray. But he could see that Ray had more than one reason for guiding the old guy for free. He loved his stories. And he had no intention of getting down to business without a diversionary chat. But fifteen minutes with no mention of Donna was wearing on Osborne. Still, he trusted Ray had a reason for the delay, so he curbed his impatience and listened.

In his youth, Gib had made a living playing jazz piano with the bands that toured the supper clubs of the northwoods before American families opted to spend their vacation dollars on Disneyland instead of aging lakeside resorts with their tiny cabins. As he traveled, Gib had soaked up the history of the region: tales of moonshine and secret tunnels, the clubs built with mob money from Chicago, the burned-out cars found deep in the woods where no roads ran. He'd heard the stories and could embellish them as well as any raconteur.

One day he discovered that the fingers so talented on the keys of the piano added dazzle when shuffling a deck of cards. That knack plus his inscrutable face added up to success as a professional poker player.

And now that poker had hit the big time, he had been drafted to play the other side of the table. Gib Salisbury was the dealer with the best eye in casino country for that big fish they all wanted to hook: the cardsharp.

Osborne leaned back in his chair, pondering the old man's remark. "Did you say we're asking the wrong questions?" He repeated Gib's words.

"Don't ask me about sore losers going after one of my trainees—ask me who tries too hard to get close? That's where the trouble lies. Let me tell you what I tell my people: 'Every table has a cheater. Your job is spot 'em and stop 'em. And if you can't do that—at least scare 'em.'

"So while the training begins with basics of the games played, the emphasis is on watching the players. You see, boys, one reason I got into poker is just that: *Nothing is more interesting than the human face.* So watch the players. It don't matter if they're wearing dark glasses, 3-D glasses, or shot glasses—keep a sharp eye.

"Miss Donna was doin' okay 'cept for her socializin' at the bar. She was way too friendly with some of the folks who've been playing here. Not that it was her fault. They was layin' it on thick. I told her so. Maybe I was crude, but I told her that poker ain't like sex. At these tables, man, you fake it—you lose.'

"What do you mean exactly?" said Osborne.

"She had to learn to keep friendship out of her job. Those people buying her drinks and talkin' so sweet. They aren't interested in Miss Donna the human being. They're just interested in a Miss Donna they can charm to look the other way when they mark a card or short the pot. I mean, these guys are amateurs, always trying the obvious: weasel the dealer.

"So what you want to know from me, boys, is not who was sore—but who was *courting* the little lady."

"Were they hitting on the other trainees, too?" said Osborne.

"Donna was the only woman in the class—our first female poker dealer."

"I see," said Osborne. "Who was it that was leaning on her?"

"Couple of fellas—regulars. They've been showing up almost every Saturday for the last three months. Into the house for so much that we've cut 'em off until they pay in a percentage of what they owe. Ed Forsyth and Parker Nehlson."

At the look on Osborne's face, Gib chuckled. "Thought maybe you'd know those boys. Everybody around here does. Those two got the same problem with alcohol as they do with gambling—they drink too much. And you can't play smart cards drunk."

"You think they're out of control?"

"Somebody does. Parker's wife won't let 'em come without that driver they got. She sends 'em over with that guy and he brings 'em home. That's smart, too. Put one of those two behind a wheel and somebody'll get killed."

"Who's the driver?"

"I dunno. He always sits on the side, plays the slots while he waits. Skinny little guy who dresses like a cowboy. Always wears the same dirty jeans, the same blue-checked flannel shirt. Bow-legged. He had a few conversations with Donna, too. But just friendly-like—not like the other two hanging all over her. The little guy—I kinda think she knew him from somewhere else."

"Anything else you can tell us about him?" said Ray. "Doesn't sound familiar to me, and I know a lot of people."

Gib nursed his soda. "Yeah, well, that driver is a strange one. He has a tattoo up his left forearm you can't miss: a praying mantis."

"So Joan Nehlson never comes to the casino herself—she sends the men over in a car," said Osborne, making a note.

   "I didn't say that," said Gib. "She doesn't come with the boys—she comes alone. Thinks she's smarter than everybody, too—though she only plays with women. Comes in on Wednesdays when we have amateur ladies poker night.

   "She's got one move and she pulls it off half the time—the bully bet. She sits down to a game of Texas Hold'em with a huge stack of chips. All the other gals are trying to keep their bets under ten dollars but she'll bet the whole stack. Out to intimidate the table."

twenty

In seeing some of the new fishermen on the old riffles, I'm reminded of a friend who told me he's recently taken up golf because he likes the clothes.

—John Merwin

Osborne swung down the narrow paved road that led toward the Forsyth and Nehlson properties, past the sign that read PRIVATE ROAD/NO TRESPASSING. Past two more signs that read PRIVATE/KEEP OUT.

He was three-quarters of a mile in when the road forked into two unpaved lanes. He knew where he was—midway up the Pickerel chain. Along this chain, the lakes could be small, some tiny, and so ringed with bogs that buildable land was at a premium.

While some people avoided the boggy acres, likely breeding grounds for mosquitoes, others preferred the remote locations and built long, long docks that extended out over the bogs to where they could launch their boats. If you wanted privacy and limited access to your property by water—this was the land for you.

A quick study of the plat book before leaving the casino parking lot had indicated that, the Nehlson name on the sign aside, it was the Garmin Family Foundation that owned significant acreage back in here. Nothing was marked as owned by Forsyth, but the plat book was out-dated by three years—enough time to buy and build.

The more Osborne saw, the more that made sense. Where the road forked, it dropped down and away, making it easy to see the rooflines of two lodge-style houses set about three hundred feet from each other. The one to the left was tiled in rust-colored shingles—a style from the thirties and forties when wealthy Chicagoans built summer mansions. The boggy lowland stretching south and east of the property offered a magnificent view of the lake beyond.

Over the bog ran a wide, planked dock, weathered gray by the elements. At the end of the dock was a pontoon that looked large enough to carry a party of thirty.

All he could see of the other house was a new roof of burgundy metal. A metal roof in the northwood has a surface slippery enough to prevent snow buildup, is guaranteed to last a hundred years—and is quite expensive. Osborne was so taken with it, he never heard the footsteps coming up from behind.

"Looking for somebody?" The voice was gruff and un-welcoming, its tone implying less a question than a suggested time of departure. The man stood off to the left of Osborne's open window, hands on his hips and arms akimbo. The sleeves of the blue-checked shirt were rolled above the elbows, and there was no missing the praying mantis gleaming black along the inside of his left forearm.

"Yes, the Nehlsons," said Osborne, starting to open his car door.

The man took two steps toward Osborne. Although he was small and skinny, the black eyes glittering under the shaggy, uncut hair were hard and uncompromising. His face—either deeply tanned or just plain filthy—was in bad need of a shave. High-heeled cowboy boots, scuffed with the toes turning up, anchored his bowed legs. The boots poking out from under worn and dusty Levi's, along with a leather-handled bowie knife strapped to his belt, gave him the appearance of a miniature outlaw.

"Not here." He yanked his thumb as he spoke. "Out. Thatta way—" The rudeness caught Osborne by surprise. He resisted an irrational urge to jump out and punch the guy.

Instead, he said, "Hey, you, back off, bud. I've got official business here with Joan and her husband." He didn't, but he could sure as hell make something up.

"I told you—*not home*." The punk stepped closer to Osborne's car, blocking him from opening the door.

"All right, all right," said Osborne. He wasn't sure if his heart was pounding from fear or fury.

"Georgy! What you got there?" A tall, broad-chested man dressed in tan golf shorts and a lavender Polo shirt came striding up the driveway from the right. The silver-gray hair was swept back and up over a high forehead that emphasized a long, bony face, tanned and smooth as if burnished with affluence.

"Trespasser," said the punk, spitting the word out. He did not back off.

Osborne decided to get out of his car and introduce himself—even if it meant banging the punk with his car door. The guy backed off just far enough—his eyes never leaving Osborne's face.

"Dr. Paul Osborne from the Loon Lake Police," said Osborne over the short man's head to the newcomer in the golf shorts. "I'm looking for the Nehlsons—Joan and Parker."

"And why would that be?" the voice slurred.

"We're investigating her sister's death and I have a few more questions. Do you mind if I ask you who you are?"

The man rocked on his feet. "Peggy's dead?" A breeze wafted the unmistakable fragrance of whiskey Osborne's way, and the man blinked hard as if trying to get past seeing double. Osborne knew that feeling.

"Yes . . ." Osborne waited, not sure how much he wanted to say if this was who he thought it was.

"S'okay, Georgy. I'll handle this. Ed Forsyth, Mr. Osborne. I'm their neighbor. Close friend."

"*Doctor* Osborne," said Osborne, correcting him. Forsyth weaved as he extended a hand. Osborne took the hand—but managed to grasp only the fingers.

"Sorry about George, but he's under orders. Sch-trict orders."

"You get a lot of people trespassing back here?" said Osborne, relieved to find a neutral subject.

"Sightseers, mostly. Now what was that you said about Joan's sister? You said she's *dead*?" Forsyth's voice squeaked on the last word.

"Yes, I did," said Osborne, crossing his arms and leaning back against his car. A crafty expression had moved into the man's eyes, and he seemed to grow more focused. It was as if he was calculating through an alcoholic haze and the numbers were coming up positive.

After watching Forsyth weigh the news in silence, Osborne said, "I'm surprised you haven't heard."

"Hell, I just drove up from the city. Got in half an hour ago. You're sure . . . she's dead?" It was the third time he asked the question. "Come on down to the house—let me offer you a drink. Martini? No, no—what am I thinking? You're on official business. Thas's right, right?" Again, the slow weave on the feet.

"Right. But thank you. Since the Nehlsons aren't here, I'll be on my way." Osborne got into his car thinking he should stay, stay and press Forsyth for information on the debacle with Peg's surgery. But the guy was so smashed. He must have been drinking the entire drive up from Milwaukee. Osborne shuddered to think that Mallory was driving the same highway.

He backed his car up and around to leave. He hadn't gone twenty yards when he saw the blue-checked shirt. The punk had heard every word and made no effort to hide. Recognizing it was a perverse urge to be polite, Osborne lifted his hand in a wave and felt a curious satisfaction when he got no response. Jerk.

The Lincoln Navigator pulled to a stop just ahead of Osborne's car. Joan was driving. She slid her window down, stuck her head out the window, and squinted toward him. "Dr. Osborne?"

"Yes, I stopped by with a few questions but you weren't in—and now I'm afraid I have a five o'clock appointment back in town."

"No, wait a minute, please." She jumped down from the big SUV and ran up to lean into his window. "Did you get the news about Ed Forsyth and his clinic?" The woman's face was moist with perspiration, causing her makeup to cake in the lines around her eyes, and he could see moist circles under the arms of her black blouse. The voice that had boomed so officiously in the morning now sounded tight, stressed.

"Just met the man. What is it?"

"Well, I had no idea and now I feel so responsible. That clinic of his has been cheating the big insurance companies—maybe even the government. We just got off the phone with our lawyer."

"You didn't know about this earlier?"

"After our meeting with you and Chief Ferris this morning, I called our family's law firm for advice on making arrangements for Peg's burial, and that's when I heard the news. The investigators have been calling his former patients. I'm on the list because I had cheek implants done there last year. When they called our home, our housekeeper put them in touch with my lawyer.

"This is so upsetting—I can't begin to tell you. I have to wonder how much poor Peg might have known about this. And it's *all my fault*," she said, emphasizing her words. "When my sister called me last year for advice on where to get a face-lift, I'm the one who insisted she see Ed."

Her eyes searched Osborne's as she leaned in even closer, forcing Osborne to lean back. "I am *so* worried. Our friend can be a desperate man when pushed. I've seen him angry . . ."

"You think the investigation may have something to do with Peg's lawsuit?" said Osborne.

Joan braced herself with both arms against Osborne's car door and dropped her head with a shake. "If I put my sister in harm's way, I'll never forgive myself."

Osborne looked past her toward the car. Parker was leaning forward from the passenger seat. He called through the window. "Joan, you better tell him the rest."

Joan stepped back from Osborne's car and crossed her arms tightly over her chest. She kicked at a stone in the road with her sandaled foot before fixing her eyes on his. "We're investors in the clinic. He tricked us. We could be liable! We could lose everything. Parker and I had no idea what he was up to . . ."

Ah, thought Osborne, so much for poor Peg's death. It was still all about Joan.

twenty-one

Fish dinners will make a man spring like a flea.

—Thomas Jordan

Osborne hurried from his car to the back door, Mike happy at his heels. It was already past five. Sure enough, the red light on his answering machine was blinking. He had three messages, the first from Mallory.

"Dad," she said, sounding more buoyant than she had in months, "I'm so sorry to call at the last minute like this— but I can't make it up after all. The funniest thing happened. I was turning in my paper for that class on Human Behavior in Organizations and walked into the building at the very same time as this totally adorable man in my study group. We were chatting about how it is to be back to school after a divorce and before I knew it—he invited me to go sailing this weekend!

"Dad—the guy is so cool. I know you'll understand. Oh, by the way, I had this long e-mail from an old friend of yours. Beebo Rowland. Her late husband, Choppy, went to boarding school with you. She wanted your phone number. Dad, that's the Rowland family who donated the new tech building to Northwestern. Definitely take some time with Mrs. Rowland—so maybe I won't have to support you in your old age. Just kidding! Love you, bye—"

The next message was from Ray. "Y-o-o-o, Doc. Gina and I are here in the office with Chief Ferris . . ." There was a long pause as if he was hoping Osborne would pick up the phone. "Okay, I give up—you are not home. Here's the deal: As I speak, we are in the process of getting Gina set up to work from here. I will then drop her by her cabin to get settled—then pick her up at six to meet you and Chief Ferris at the Loon Lake Pub for fish fry. You catch up with us there. Six-fifteen."

In the background as he spoke, Osborne could hear a buzz of women's voices. He hit the button for the third and final message.

"Paul . . ." said a voice, ingratiating, mellifluous. "This is a friend from your past. It hasn't been easy to find you, dear. Your darling daughter, Mallory, gave me this number." He listened hard, hoping to hear a hint of the exuberant twelve-year-old girl he had known so long ago.

"I'm staying at the Dairyman's in Boulder Junction this weekend. With friends. I was hoping you might join us for cocktails tomorrow evening. Mallory e-mailed that you are widowed now—so am I. It would be so lovely to catch up with one another."

She spoke like a queen, not a kid, and left a phone number. It fit that Beebo would be staying at the private resort. The Dairyman's had long been a haven for wealthy families from Chicago.

Osborne studied the phone for a long minute. Then he called the number she left. To his relief, an answering machine picked up. His message was brief: This was a busy weekend, and much as he would enjoy renewing their friendship, it would have to wait. "Put me on your guest list, Beebo, for the next time you're up north. I am sure we can work something out then." Good, that was over.

He threw Mike's bowl down with such haste that the

dog scrambled for the morsels spilling across the kitchen floor. Osborne filled his water dish, slopped that on the floor as well, then dashed for the shower.

He swung by the police department but saw no sign of Lew's cruiser. She must have found the time to go home and change. Since he was a few minutes early, he parked and walked in. Marlene, who shared the switchboard position with her daughter-in-law, Fern, was off. Fern was on.

She was a younger version of Marlene—just as vivacious and dedicated. "Yep, she's all set up in the large conference room," said Fern in answer to his question about Gina and her computer. "The door is locked right now—do you need me to open it?"

"No, no—but did they say if they would be back to work later this evening?"

"I don't think so," said Fern. "Last I heard from Chief Ferris, she's planning to be in first thing in the morning. Roger and Todd are on tonight. Jeez Louise—we're all just so happy that darn Country Fest is over tomorrow. This has been one wild week."

The Loon Lake Pub was packed when Osborne got there. But Ray, who had once shared his special beer-battered haddock recipe with the chef, had managed to snag a table for four. He was waiting with Gina when Osborne arrived.

"Doc!" Gina jumped to her feet. Gina Palmer was a petite woman with a cap of short black hair, quite straight, that set off her white skin and framed a pair of black eyes that snapped with humor and intelligence. As often as he had seen her, Osborne had never known her not to wear black, and tonight was no exception. She looked like a tiny dynamo in a long-sleeved black knit shirt over slim black pants.

Gina Palmer's first trip to the northwoods had been to

help Lew and Osborne investigate the murder of one of her close friends two years earlier, and she had fallen in love with the lake country. Or maybe it was the guy with the stuffed fish on his head. Whatever the reason, she was now the proud owner of a cabin on Loon Lake: an excellent excuse to visit at least four times a year.

"I hear you're all set up and ready to help us out tomorrow," said Osborne as he pulled out his chair.

"Hey, Doc, our queen of the digital crumbs has already had a breakthrough," said Ray with quiet pride. "Go ahead, tell Doc what you told me and Chief Ferris."

Gina glanced around the tables nearby, then pulled her chair in closer to Osborne's. She had a voice packed in gravel and tended to fire words at you in an unrelenting staccato, which may have been the secret to her success at driving teams of investigative reporters.

"Doc, I'm a teaching fellow in the Life Sciences Communications Department at the University of Wisconsin–Madison this term. So when Ray called yesterday about the lawsuit that your victim was planning to file, I called a former colleague of mine who heads up the special projects investigative reporting team at the *Milwaukee Journal Sentinel*.

"When he got on the line and I said I was looking for some background on a plastic surgeon by the name of Edward Forsyth, the first thing he said to me was 'Are you calling because of what happened yesterday?' And he wanted to know how I heard about it.

"Well, y'know, I had no idea what he was talking about. So I told him I was doing a friend a favor. Just a check to see if they had any stories on the doctor or his clinic, since it's located in that area. That's when my friend said that one of his reporters had received an anonymous tip involving insurance fraud by the clinic yesterday morning. A phone call. Then this morning the same reporter got an envelope containing a list of the names and phone numbers of dozens of clinic patients.

"The reporter called the FBI's health fraud unit and talked to a source there—they got the same tip. The way things look right now, Forsyth's clinic may be shut down over the weekend. If I know the Feds, they'll want to raid the place by surprise so they can get hard drives before anyone tampers with them."

"What kind of fraud—did the reporter say?" said Osborne, remembering Joan Nehlson's sweaty armpits.

While Gina was talking, Lew had come into the restaurant and taken the chair to Osborne's left. Off-duty and out of uniform, she looked radiant, crisp and refreshed in jeans and an open-collared orange shirt that set off her tan. She indicated with a quick wave that he should pay attention to the rest of what Gina had to say.

"Criminal charges could be filed as early as next week against Forsyth, two physicians he employs, and his chief administrator for fraudulent insurance claims. It seems the clinic has been recruiting people for procedures they didn't need such as colonoscopies, endoscopies, and an unusual, very expensive procedure for sweaty palms. Each recruit would have all three of the procedures and the clinic would bill their insurers for tens of thousands of dollars.

"In return, the recruit got either a cash payment or discounts on tummy tucks, breast enhancement, or having their eyelids done. The envelope that arrived in the mail this morning contained the names of some two hundred recruits—more than a dozen from northern Wisconsin."

"I wonder if Peg Garmin was on that list?" said Osborne.

"No. But both her friends were—Donna Federer and Pat Kuzynski."

"I checked with the families late this afternoon," said Lew, chiming in. "Ralph knew nothing, of course. But Pat's mother said she thought Pat had the tests done because she needed them. From the tone of her voice, I could tell she'd been hoping we wouldn't find out. How do you explain a stripper from Thunder Bay needing surgery for sweaty palms?"

"The question I have," said Ray, "is who's the tipster?" He looked around the table with a sheepish expression. "At least that's what I always ask the warden when he catches me on private water."

"And does he tell you?" said Lew with a knowing grin.

"Of course not—but I always have a pretty good idea. It's the guy who hasn't caught a walleye over three pounds in his lifetime and is jealous as hell."

"Seriously, Gina," said Osborne, "who do they think called in the tip?"

"My experience over twenty years of investigative reporting—it's almost always a disgruntled employee," she said. "Ninety-nine percent of the time that's who blows the whistle."

"How about a disgruntled financial partner?" said Osborne. And he related Joan Nehlson's worry that she and her husband as investors in the clinic could be held accountable.

"Not unless it can be proven that they knew what was going on," said Gina. "Now, if they were actively involved in recruiting patients for the procedures—that's all the proof the authorities will need. But it is certainly not a crime to recommend a plastic surgeon to your sister.

"I have a question, though. Did Peg Garmin know about

the fraud and if so—was she threatening to expose the scheme as part of her lawsuit?"

The table was quiet, then Lew said, "Ray, you may be right after all—Peg was the target. But Donna and Pat, if they had agreed to be witnesses, may well have put themselves at risk for the same reason. However, whoever shot those women, it wasn't Dr. Edward Forsyth. The man was miles away at the time the victims were murdered."

Osborne looked over at Lew in surprise. "So you've been able to fix the time of death?"

"Better than that," said Lew with enthusiasm as she reached for the appetizer tray and helped herself to a cracker with the Pub's famous liver spread. Osborne watched as she munched away happily, the muted lighting in the restaurant causing her dark eyes to glow amber.

As the waitress appeared to hand around drinks to the table—ginger ale to Osborne and Ray, frosty mugs of Leininkugel Original to the women—Osborne reached sideways to give Lew's shoulders a light, quick hug. "You look stunning tonight," he whispered.

"Thank you, Doc," she said with a pleased smile. "Believe me, it helps that it's been a very good day—which I deserve after a very tough week. A toast . . ." She raised her glass and everyone else followed suit: "To everyone here at the table. What has been accomplished over the last two days could never have happened without the help of each of you."

"Sorry, Doc," said Lew. "I'll answer your question on the time of death in a minute. It's just that I'm starving— forgot to eat lunch after you and Ray left for the casino." She reached for more crackers, spread each with the liver paté, and chewed with delight before continuing.

"Okay," she said, dusting cracker crumbs from her

hands, "I had a visit from Robbie Mikkleson with the results of the data recorder from Peg's car. Bruce was so excited to hear what they found, he jumped right in his car and drove up from Wausau this afternoon to check it out."

"Excuse us for a minute," said Ray, rising from his chair. "We heard about this earlier, and if you two don't mind, I see some friends that I would like Gina to meet."

"Sure, go right ahead," said Lew. She turned her attention back to Osborne, took a swig of her beer, then said, "So the three of us—myself, Robbie, and Bruce—drove out to the site where car was found.

"First, Bruce was able to confirm that a bungee cord found on the ground near the car is the one that was tied to the bottom of the steering wheel and the arm of the brake pedal to keep the car moving in a straight line. Robbie's mechanic friend put the data from the car through the computer, which showed that the cruise control had been set for sixty, though the car had reached just forty-six miles per hour when it rolled.

"So we have someone somewhere who thought they had that car headed straight down the road and into the pines where the road makes that sharp turn—and jumped out as soon as they could get the cruise control to resume. Their error was eyeballing that road. It looks pretty darn straight but it isn't exact—add the rough surface and you have a car that ran off too soon, hit a boulder hidden under that stand of tag alders, and rolled.

"If it had done what it was supposed to do—hit those trees at sixty miles an hour—there would have been very few questions. Even Bruce said there would have been such severe trauma to the bodies that we wouldn't have known to look for bullet wounds. Drunk driving, a missed turn—no evidence of murder."

A funny look came over Lew's face as she was speaking. She looked over Osborne's head, then raised a finger to her lips just as he felt a hand on his shoulder.

"Beebo!" It had been fifty years, but he recognized the laughing eyes instantly.

twenty-two

Fishing consists of a series of misadventures interspersed by occasional moments of glory.

—Howard Marshall, *Reflections on a River*

The woman who hovered over him seemed tall, wide, and shining. She was deeply tanned with short, spiky, light brown hair tipped gold. Golden globes hung from her ears, a gold chain encircled her neck, and gold bracelets on both arms jangled as she spoke. He resisted the urge to warn her against going in the water with all that hardware.

"Paul! This is such a coincidence. I just left a message on your answering machine today! And now to run into you here? Well, I'll be—"

Napkin in hand, Osborne scrambled to his feet. He gave the woman a hearty handshake as he said, "Yes, Beebo. I got your message an hour ago—"

"Well, I certainly hope you're available tomorrow," she said before he could finish. Then she looked down at Lew, who was watching with a bemused smile on her face. "Hello, I'm a childhood friend of Paul's—Beebo Rowland. We knew each other as kids, didn't we, Paul.

"I lost my husband two years ago. This year I made it a goal to track down all my old friends and make a new life.

Paul was one of my first targets—and it has not been easy to find this man. Paul, you're not on-line!"

"No, I—"

"Well, at least your children are, thank goodness. Now, I don't want to keep you and your friend here—"

"Oh, I'm sorry. Beebo, I'd like you to meet Lewellyn Ferris—"

"How nice to meet you, Lewellyn. Now, Paul, I must get back to my friends, but tomorrow evening at six at the main lodge at the Dairyman's. See you then?"

"No, I'm sorry, Beebo—I have a commitment tomorrow evening." He knew better than to say he was going fishing.

"No, Doc, you go right ahead. We can get together another time," said Lew.

Beebo looked from one to the other, then said, "How about brunch instead? If you have plans, don't change those, Paul. We have so much to catch up on. I want to see you when we can take our time. How about tomorrow morning at ten—same place. They have a lovely brunch at the Dairyman's."

"Well—"

"Fine. I will see you then. Enjoy dinner, you two," said Beebo. Then, with a clap of her hands, she said, "This is absolutely my favorite spot for a real Northwoods fish fry. Don't you just love it?" And she was gone as quickly as she had arrived.

Lew leaned forward with a teasing look in her eye. "And what was it you were up to at age twelve with that attractive woman, Doc?"

"I was fourteen, she was twelve." Just then Ray and Gina returned to the table. "Can we discuss her at another time?" said Osborne, feeling the redness creeping up his neck.

"Oh, I think we must," said Lew as her plate of beer-battered fish was set down in front of her. "I can't wait to hear all about her. You know what they say, Doc—first love, best love."

Osborne thought that over for a second, then said, "You made that up, Lewellyn." She laughed and reached for the pepper.

Osborne had to admit: He wasn't that unhappy that he would be seeing Beebo tomorrow. He could see her at a table across the room with two other couples. Even from a distance, she had a vibrancy unusual for a woman in her early sixties. It would be fun to catch up.

Though the food was good, they did not linger. Given the crowd, they were lucky to be served and get their check before seven-thirty.

"Chief, you're still up for stopping out at the Happy Daze Pub tonight, right?" said Ray.

"You better believe it," said Lew. "Thought you said that the woman who served Peg and the girls Wednesday would be tending bar tonight?"

"That's what the owner told me this morning. Said she'd give her a call and make sure she knew we'd be by."

Terri Schultz had been tending bar at the Happy Daze Pub for six years. Osborne recognized her face though her name hadn't rung a bell. A short, chubby woman, Terri wore her red-brown hair pulled back in a ponytail, a shapeless red sweatshirt, and black jeans. Since the bar served pizza and sandwiches, she was constantly taking off and putting on a soiled white chef's apron.

The two gas pumps outside were self-serve so she didn't have to fuss with anything except the cash and credit cards. The pumps plus lottery tickets plus fishing licenses kept Terri and the other bartender busy.

They took stools at the bar and waited for Terri to finish with a customer. It was a moderately busy night, and as they waited, Osborne remembered what it was that made Terri distinctive: She had a collection of very dirty jokes that she told with relish and a hearty laugh. She was a pleasant woman who made it easy for strangers to linger and listen.

Tonight she was ready to take time with Ray and his party between breaks serving and bantering with her regulars.

"Yep, yep," she had said when they first got there, "you got it. Those girls stopped by here every Wednesday on their way home. Got a kick out of those three—we called 'em 'the karaoke kids.' Every Wednesday 'cept January when we close down for a month. Cute, those three. Hate hearing what happened, doncha know. Just makes you wonder. What kinda weirdos do we have around here?" She slammed her dishrag on the counter and gave it an angry swipe.

"So they were here this Wednesday late, right?"

"Yep. The usual. They shared a pizza and a pitcher of beer and gassed up. They always filled the tank of that pretty little convertible and split the cost. Three ways— same's they did every week."

"Who else was here? Anybody unusual? Anybody talk to the women?"

Terri thought hard. "Well, down at this end I had 'pepperoni, black olives, and no onions'—he's a regular. Nice guy. Carpenter, I think. Over at that table were Jeff Kapelski and his old man having a couple beers after fishing. They'll be in later tonight, too, if you wanna talk to 'em.

This was late, y'know, and I was in the kitchen working on the books. About eleven-thirty.

"Hold on a minute—Lizzie!" She called down to the other bartender, a slim, fresh-faced blonde who looked about thirteen, though her extremely close fitting jeans and black halter top made it obvious she was older.

Lizzie walked down the bar and Terri repeated the question, then said, "Anybody you notice?"

"Yeah, mantis man was hanging around. Now that you ask—he's been here the last few Wednesdays. Comes in about eleven usually."

"What do you mean 'mantis man'?" said Lew.

"Oh, he's this guy who has a praying mantis tattooed down his arm. Kind of a cute guy, started coming in this summer. Name's George."

"Oh, sure, I know who you mean," said Terri. "Quiet guy. At least, he's never had much to say when I've been around."

"So what did he do Wednesday?" said Lew. "Have a couple beers and leave?"

"That's what he usually did—but this Wednesday, after he left, he came back to make a phone call. I know because I had to get him some change. He was pretty upset over something, too."

"Was this before or after the women came in?" said Lew.

"Both. He got here before they did, left right after 'em. Fact, he was talking to the tall one as they walked out the door. They seemed to know each other."

"Was he sitting with them?"

"Oh no, he stayed down at that end of the bar. Like I said before, he left when they did and later came running in to make that phone call." She pointed to the pay phone on the wall near the restrooms.

"Any idea how long was he gone?"

"Oh, gee . . ." said Lizzie, jamming her hands into her back pockets as she tried to remember. "Well, we close at one. So for sure he was back before then. I gave him the change, then I was down at the other end of the bar washing glasses so I wasn't listening until he started cursing."

"Any chance you heard what he said then?"

"Oh, yeah—his language was so bad, I walked down to tell him to put a lid on it, y'know. That's when I heard him say a couple things like 'What the hell do you expect me to do with three thousand pounds?' Then he made reference to just what they could do with it themselves. Like 'shove it,' y'know?" Lizzie was hesitant to repeat exactly what he had said.

"Shove three thousand pounds, you mean?" said Lew.

"Right. But then he calmed down and I heard him say, 'Okay, okay, but I'll do it tomorrow—I don't have anything with me to make that happen tonight.' "

Both Lew and Gina had been taking notes while Lizzie talked. Now Gina walked over to write down the number of the pay phone.

"What else do you know about him, Lizzie?" said Lew. "Any idea what kind of car he drives? His last name? 'Bout how old do you think he is?"

Lizzie shook her head and said, "Oh, gosh, early thirties. Maybe older. He's got that weather-beaten look so it's hard to tell. Don't know his last name—only know he's George 'cause I asked him once. He drives an old, dark blue pickup."

"Big, medium, or little like a Toyota?"

"Big. Like a Ford, kinda."

"Lizzie, this is a big help," said Lew. "If you remember anything else he may have said that night, or any night, will you call me right away? Or if he walks in here later tonight—call me immediately. Here's where I can be reached."

Lizzie looked down at the card Lew handed her, then said, "Is there something wrong with this guy? He's real cute."

"We don't know yet. But he may have been one of the last people to see the women before they were killed so I'd like to ask him some questions."

A quick check with the other patrons in the bar turned up nothing. No one knew anything more about George than the two bartenders. None of the men had even noticed him.

Lew started for the door then stopped and walked back to the bar. "One last question, Terri," she said. "Any idea why those women would have taken the dead highway home?"

"Oh sure," said Terri. "I'm the one told 'em that short-cut. First time they stopped in here. They always went that way—cuts fifteen minutes off getting to Loon Lake. Have to watch for deer and it might get your car a little dusty, but you get back to town good and fast."

"A guy with a praying mantis on his arm—that's a fashion statement," said Gina as she opened the door of the bar to head outside. "I think I prefer Ray's hat." Osborne was right behind her. He turned around, anxious for Lew to get out of the bar.

"I know the guy," said Osborne, the minute Lew stepped through the bar's screen door. "The guy with the praying mantis—he's the caretaker for Ed Forsyth and the Nehlsons. I ran into him out there today. *Not* very friendly."

"Has to be the same guy that my buddy at the casino

told us about," said Ray. "The one that drives Forsyth and Nehlson to the casino."

"Why would he do that?" said Gina.

"So they can drink and not worry about getting picked up," said Ray. "I wouldn't be surprised if one or both those two aren't close to losing their drivers' license if they got stopped—this state is tough on drunk drivers. That's my guess, anyway."

Lew had pulled out her cell phone and was checking her notepad. She found what she was looking for and punched in a phone number.

"Are you thinking what I'm thinking?" said Osborne as she waited for someone to pick up.

"Very likely," said Lew, listening. "I want the guy's name and where he lives so we can check the tread marks we picked up on the road near where the women were killed . . ." She quit the call and punched in the number again. "Match those tread marks against this George fellow's tires. Trying the Nehlsons right now . . ."

The phone kept ringing. "No answer." Lew snapped her phone closed.

twenty-three

It is not a fish until it is on the bank.

—Irish proverb

Osborne was in baby food on his way to coffee when he rounded the corner of the aisle and nearly bumped into Pauline Leffterholz and her short-shorts boyfriend. His first inclination was to duck past the end cap of potato chips in hopes of not being seen, but it was too late. Pauline spotted him.

"Doc?" she said, her tobacco voice reverberating in the empty aisles. It was ten minutes before closing time at the Loon Lake Market and they had to be the only customers left. Osborne had remembered, as he drove through town after saying good night to everyone and arranging to meet Lew at six the next morning, that he was out of coffee! Of all the bad habits he had managed to give up, caffeine was not one.

Darn. If not for that addiction, he wouldn't be here—likely to be trapped into a conversation he'd just as soon avoid. Pauline hurried toward him, the boyfriend close behind. Osborne could swear he was still in the same shorts. At least they fit the same.

"Anything new?" said Pauline in a tone so flat Osborne knew that wasn't her real question. "They're releasing

Patsy's body tomorrow and I've arranged for the funeral to be held on Wednesday. Since you've known our family all these years and you were there to help when they found Patsy—I was hoping you might be one of the pallbearers. Fred here's in charge."

Too tired to come up with an excuse and well aware it would hurt her feelings if he did, Osborne said, "It would be a privilege, Pauline. Fred, I don't believe we've met," he said, extending his hand. Short Shorts gave a grunt and returned the gesture.

"So, hey now," said Fred, "sounds like that doctor they was all seein' is a crook. So you guys better be in the process of investigating that sucker, right?"

If Fred needed to impress Pauline by telling the Loon Lake Police how to do their job, Osborne had no intention of getting in his way. "Yep, you got that right," he said, hoping that might be where he could end this conversation.

"So nothin' else new, though, huh?" Pauline looked so sad.

Osborne had a sudden sense that she was already resigned to never knowing who murdered her daughter. That Pat Kuzynski was one of those women whose lives didn't matter a whole hell of a lot to many people. That her death would be forgotten as soon as a more important crime came along to demand the attention of Lew and the limited manpower of the Loon Lake Police.

"Well, Pauline, we just got a new lead tonight. We're looking for a fellow whom we know saw them shortly before . . . he's got an unusual tattoo on his arm. A praying mantis." Osborne did his best to make her feel better. "Ever hear of such a thing?"

"Oh, hey, I know the guy," said Fred. "You're talkin' 'bout Little George Buchholz. Shows up at Nub's Pub every now and then—not a bad pool player neither. We like to call him Lil' Georgy." Fred snorted. "He don't like that much.

"Yep, George's got that praying mantis on his arm, all right. Says it's a symbol for patience. If you ask me, he needs a symbol for funny business. Guy's got no sense of humor."

"Buchholz is the name?" said Osborne. "How do you spell that? Any idea where he lives?"

"Buchholz, jes' like it sounds."

"Okay." Osborne resisted rolling his eyes. He could think of three spelling variations right off the bat.

"Last I knew he had a house in that block up behind the junior high. He's the kinda guy does a little of everything, y'know? Some plumbing, some wiring. I think he mentioned he was fixing the place up to sell. You want to find him—look him up in the phone book."

Which was exactly what Osborne did.

One night short of full, the moon was bright enough to pick up the blue on the outside of the frame house. It looked like any old house under repair: Plastic was stretched across some windows, the front porch roof was half-finished, the yard was littered with odds and ends of equipment. Off in one corner was a fishing boat on a rusted trailer, its tarp cover ripped and hanging off one end. But no sign of a dark blue truck.

Osborne parked and got out of his car. He saw no light in any of the windows. Up on the front porch, he pressed a buzzer but heard no ringing inside, so he banged on the door. No answer. He walked around the house to the back. An ancient stone garage, its walls crumbling and roof sagging took up half the yard. No truck here either.

A neighbor's dog barked and he heard a door slamming. He walked back to the front of the house. He recognized the next-door neighbor who had just turned on a yard light as he let his dog out. It was a friend of his son-in-law Mark's.

"Larry?" Osborne called across the yard.

"Hey, Dr. Osborne, what are you doing over there?"

"I'm trying to find your neighbor. Does George Buchholz live here?"

"Unfortunately. Look at that place. Makes the whole neighborhood look bad."

"Well—any idea where I might find him?"

Larry stepped off his porch and walked across the lawn. He lowered his voice, "He's working for some people up near Manitowish, I believe. Managing their properties, is what he told me. But I don't really know. George is a difficult man to talk to. Hasn't been around much these last couple weeks."

"So no wife and family living here?"

"That guy?" Larry gave a harsh laugh. "Warm and fuzzy does not apply to my neighbor. Trust me. My wife and I have a hard time working up the courage to ask him to keep his lawn mowed."

With a sweep of his right arm that encompassed his neighbor's house and yard, Larry shook his head in disgust as he said, "Do you believe that place? See the front porch with all that plastic in the windows? See the crap in the yard? Guy always does the job halfway. Nothing is ever finished. Hurts our property values, y'know."

Climbing back in his car, Osborne regretted for the umpteenth time not investing in a cell phone. He couldn't call Lew until he got home. When he finally did reach her, he could tell he was waking her up.

"I got the name of our man with the tattoo," he said, determined not to take any more time than necessary. "Talked to one of his neighbors. He lives alone and is not one to attend neighborhood block parties—know what I mean?"

"Tell you what, Doc," said Lew, her voice drowsy. "Do me a favor and ask Ray to stop by that house in the morning and shoot some photos of whatever tire tracks he can find on the property. Even without the truck being there, he might get some good impressions that we can compare to the casts made by the Wausau boys."

"Will do. Are you sure you want to get going at six, Lew? Why not sleep in a little? You've been putting in sixteen-hour days."

"Not on your life. We need to beat the Country Fest crowd. By ten tomorrow morning, every highway in the county will be gridlock."

twenty-four

*No angler merely watches nature in a passive way. He en-
ters into its very existence.*

John Bailey, *Reflections on the Water's Edge*

They parked Osborne's car in the Pole Cat parking lot
after deciding to continue on in Lew's cruiser. The weather
report on WXPR as they drove up promised a sunny day
and clear skies that night, which lifted Osborne's spirits.
Tonight was the night of the full moon, the night he and
Lew were hoping to spend in float tubes with fly rods.

As Osborne slipped into the seat on the passenger side,
Lew said, "You haven't forgotten our plans, have you?"

"You must be kidding."

"Well, Doc, with a new woman in your life . . ." Again
that teasing grin. Was she really worried about Beebo? Osborne was flattered.

He settled back as Lew pulled off the highway and onto
the paved road leading to the Nehlson and Forsyth properties. They hadn't gone far when a dark green pickup truck
came around a bend toward them. Lew flashed her head-
lights, then pulled alongside.

"Good morning," she said, "I'm Chief Lewellyn Ferris
with the Loon Lake Police. Mind if I ask you your name
and what you're doing back here?"

"Not at all," said the bearded young man behind the wheel. "Mrs. Nehlson called me late last night to come out and do some cutting for her. I'm Mike Hagen, Chief Ferris. I do work for the folks back here off and on. You know, log a few trees, haul trash, keep 'em plowed in the winter. Why—is there something wrong?"

"No," said Lew, "just curious. Up pretty early to cut a few trees, aren't you?"

A flash of anxiety cramped the man's face as he answered, "She told me she wanted me here at daybreak. Insisted on it. Left a note on my door last night to make sure I got here. When that lady wants something done, she wants it done. Sure wish she paid me that fast."

"Okay, no problem, Mike. You go on ahead."

"Oh," he said, looking relieved, "well, if you're goin' in to see the Nehlsons—good luck. I sure didn't see anybody around."

"Say," said Osborne, leaning forward, "you don't happen to have that note she left with you by any chance?"

"Yeah—right here." Mike reached onto the dashboard of his truck and waved a piece of paper.

"Mind if I take a look?" said Osborne.

"You can *have* the damn thing," said Mike. He handed it to Lew, who passed it along to Osborne. She waved to Mike as he drove on out.

"What's that about the note?" she said, giving Osborne a curious look.

"I like to study people's handwriting," said Osborne. "A hobby I've had since I was a kid. Didn't you ever read those books on how you can analyze a personality through their longhand?"

"Honestly, Doc. This ranks up there with your trying to use hypnosis to relax your patients."

"C'mon, Lewellyn," said Osborne, struggling for sternness. "That worked on two people. Bear with me on this."

Lew gave him a dim eye.

He examined the note Joan Nehlson had written. She was one of those people who jotted in a half-print, half-script pattern. It looked familiar. He tried to remember where he'd seen something similar . . . felt like it had been recently, too. After a few seconds of trying, he gave up. But he tucked the note into his wallet.

They drove past the fork in the road toward the Nehlsons' lodge. Lew pulled off to the side of the big circle drive and parked. The morning sun was rising over the pines behind them, casting beams of sunlight across silvery mosses.

An expanse of new-mown lawn ran from the house down to the bog's edge. Like baby Christmas trees, miniature black spruce dotted the hummocks, which extended as far as they could see to the east. Beyond the low, flat bog was a shimmer of sky blue water. "Gorgeous view," said Lew.

"Mosquito farm," said Osborne. Beautiful as they were, he was not a fan of bogs. He didn't like the surprises beneath: pockets of deep water that could ruin a deer hunter's day; muck that could suck you in up to your knees if not your waist and ruin good boots in the process.

They walked across the driveway toward the front door of the big house. Lew knocked and they waited, but no one came to the door. "I guess Mike was right," said Lew. Osborne followed her over to the four-car garage that was attached to one side of the home. A door on one side was windowed and she peered through.

"No Lincoln Navigator," she said. "There's a sports car here."

"No dark blue truck that I can see," said Osborne.

"I guess we'll have to give it up and send you on to your lady friend early, Doc," said Lew.

"You want to try Forsyth?" said Osborne. "Right around the corner."

"Not yet. Since I'm likely to be interrogating the man in the next day or two, I'd just as soon wait until I have all the details from the investigations in Milwaukee," said Lew.

"How about I walk down the drive and see if he knows where the Nehlsons might be?"

Just then the front door opened and Parker Nehlson stepped out on the porch. He was in a brown bathrobe, his hair uncombed. He looked as if he had just gotten out of bed. Pulling the belt on the bathrobe tighter, he said, "Was that you ringing the doorbell?"

"Yes, good morning," said Lew, her voice cheery. "I am so sorry. I think we woke you up. Is Joan here? We have a few questions for you folks."

"Joan?" Parker glanced back behind him. "Joan!" he called again and waited. "No, I guess she isn't—she's not here." His wife's absence seemed to surprise him.

"Any idea when she'll be back?" said Lew.

"Golly," said Parker, running his hand through his hair. "I really don't know. She never goes anywhere this early. Maybe she's next door—having coffee with Ed. Want me to call over there?"

"That would be helpful," said Lew, crossing her arms and leaning back against the porch railing.

Parker disappeared back inside the house for a few minutes, then stepped out again. "No answer over there. Don't know what's up."

"Okay, thank you for trying," said Lew. She started to walk away, then stopped to say, "By the way, George who works for you. Where can we find him?"

"He's usually here," said Parker. "Stays in the apartment over the garage rather than drive all the way back to his place. Isn't his truck parked on the other side of the drive?"

"Not that I can see," said Lew.

"Jeez, I don't know," said Parker, appearing more mystified by the moment. "Wait a minute, let me check something." He walked down the porch to the front of the house, disappeared around the corner, then came back. "The pontoon's gone. They must be out on the lake."

"Early-morning fishing. Good day for it," said Osborne.

Again Parker shook his head. "I dunno about that—my wife hates to fish."

twenty-five

Scholars have long known that fishing eventually turns men into philosophers. Unfortunately, it is almost impossible to buy decent tackle on a philosopher's salary.

—Patrick F. McManus

Osborne walked in to find Beebo chatting with friends in the lobby of the Dairyman's main lodge.

"Oh, Paul, I'm so glad you could make it," she said, extending both arms as she strode across the room to give him a full hug and a peck on the check. Once again she struck him as looking golden—dressed in slacks and a long-sleeved shirt of a tawny color that matched her hair. She was tall and angular with a bone structure emphasized by the jewelry she was wearing.

"This way, dear," she said, pulling him into the dining room. They took a seat at a table along the windows looking over the lake. Placing her elbows on the table, Beebo steepled her fingers and rested her chin on the peak. With smiling eyes, she said, "Paul, never would I have guessed years ago what an extraordinarily good-looking man you would become."

"Thank you, Beebo," said Osborne, shifting his eyes away from hers and hoping she wouldn't go on too long.

He was not going to deny that he had a certain distinguished appearance: His black hair was silvered at the temples and, brushed back, was as full and wavy as it had been at the age of thirteen. And at six feet three inches of height, he prided himself on his erect carriage and the flat stomach that eluded so many of his peers. Add to that his Métis heritage of sculpted cheekbones, black eyes, and a deepening summer tan. He was fortunate in his genes and forever thankful. No, he did not look bad for a man in his early sixties. And embarrassed though he might feel, Osborne was happy she noticed.

"You've weathered the years quite well yourself, Beebo," he said, opening the menu. Though now that he had a chance to see her up close in the daylight, it was evident she had spent a lot of time in the sun. She had one of those permanent tans, which was emphasized by the extreme whiteness of her teeth. And when she smiled, her smile lines didn't crinkle and curve through the contours of her face. It was as if that emotion had been relegated to the lower half of her face, where it was punctuated with those teeth startlingly bright.

Osborne chastised himself: Only a dentist would be so critical.

". . . and so we raised our children in Kenilworth—just a few blocks from my mom and dad," Beebo was saying as Osborne struggled to focus on her words instead of her lower jaw.

"Oh, Kenilworth?" he interrupted her. "By chance did you ever run into the Garmins—Hugo and his wife?"

"Paul, please," said Beebo. "Remember, I'm a year younger than you. The senior Garmins were quite a bit older than Bob and I. Of course I knew them. They went to our church and Mrs. Garmin was in the Garden Club, an emeritus member. Her daughter, Joan, has been a member, too. My little sister went to North Shore Country Day with Joan. Why?"

"Well, you'll be surprised to hear that I've been working part-time since retiring from my dental practice," said Osborne. "The Loon Lake Police hire me from time to time. My background in forensic dentistry, you know."

"So you're a police officer?"

"Oh no—just a deputy. Beebo, we have a case on our hands right now that you might find interesting. The Garmins' older daughter, Peg, was found murdered earlier this week."

"You mean Mary Margaret. Oh . . . my . . . gosh," said Beebo, her eyes widening. "But, you know, the rumors about her ever since she was a kid—you always knew something bad was going to happen."

"What did you hear?"

"She was wild. Hung out with the wrong kind of guys before she ran off. Later we heard she was a hooker in Chicago. Far cry from Joan, I'll tell you. Joan, the perfect child—according to her mother, of course." Beebo gave a mock shudder. "That woman was something else.

"I'll never forget my sister, Tory, coming home from an overnight at their house in tears. Mrs. Garmin had told Tory that *she* would never get into Northwestern and be asked to join the Kappas—like Joan was sure to. 'You just don't have what it takes,' she told Tory. So condescending. Of course, what it took was a pushy mother like Mrs. Garmin.

"And you know, Paul, I am happy to say that in the long run she was wrong. Joan didn't get into Northwestern and she was never invited to be a Kappa. I've always wondered how her mother handled that. At least she managed to marry the man her mother picked out for her."

Beebo looked into Osborne's eyes. "I wish I was a better person and could tell you I feel sorry for her, but to be perfectly honest, Joan's got what she deserved. Just like her mother, she is a snob and a know-it-all. It reached a point in the Garden Club that I refused to be on any committee she was on—a lot of my friends, too. Life's too short, Paul, just too short to put up with people like Joan Nehlson. Though I do feel a little sorry for her—she's toed the line for that mother of hers and still come out on the short end."

Beebo leaned forward and dropped her voice. "I don't think she's very attractive either. For all the work she's had done. Have you met her?"

"Yesterday for a brief time. Her husband seems nice enough," said Osborne, raising his fork over the omelet and slices of Nueske's bacon that had just been placed in front of him.

"Nice but not very bright," said Beebo. "Frat boy type. You know the kind I mean—as kids they always had the new sports car, always drank too much and promptly wrecked it. In college they pledged the animal house. And when it was time for a career, they went into the family business because no one else would hire them."

"Is that what Parker did?"

"Uh-huh. His grandfather made their money in railroads and built a small train museum in honor of himself, I guess. Parker has been director of the museum for as long as I've known him. Though I hear that may be coming to an end."

She paused, then waved her fork over her plate of pancakes and said, "I'm being unfair. When Bob and I would run into the Nehlsons at social events, Parker has always been sweet to me. It's Joan I have a problem with. She's pushy and such a social climber, which is what my mother always said about her mother. Family tradition, I guess.

Poor Parker. I'll bet you anything he gets the brunt of it in that household."

"That's all very interesting," said Osborne. "You know they have quite a nice piece of property on the Pickerel chain about half an hour from here."

"Not for long they don't."

"What do you mean?"

"Word is they're close to bankrupt. Joan inherited quite a bit of money when the old man died but she gambled it all on tech stocks a few years back. Lost millions. We don't think she ever told her mother either. I mean, would you? So when the old lady died six months ago, Joan got a very rude awakening. Her mother left her share of the Garmin fortune to the church and nothing to Joan."

"That's not exactly true," said Osborne. "Peg got forty-eight million dollars."

Beebo looked at him. "You must be kidding."

"No," said Osborne. "Forty-eight million dollars."

"Well, well, well—she must have had a reason for that," said Beebo. "I do know that after Hugo died, Mrs. Garmin became much more active in our church. She attended early Mass every day of the week. Do you suppose she felt guilty for how she treated Mary Margaret years ago?"

"What makes you say that?"

"We always had the impression that Mrs. Garmin tried to avoid the fact they had an older daughter. Never talked about her."

"Beebo," said Osborne. "As a child, Peg was a victim of sexual abuse. Did you know that?"

"No!" said Beebo. She stared at Osborne, stunned. "Well, Mrs. Garmin would never have admitted to any such thing happening in their household—that I know for sure. That's the way Joan is, too. When things go wrong, it's always someone else's fault."

"Funny you say that Joan hid her financial losses from her mother," said Osborne. "Sounds like hiding bad news was a family tradition."

"I'm shocked, Paul. Forty-eight million dollars to Mary Margaret? Ohmygod, with all the financial problems they're having, Joan must be going berserk. I know their Kenilworth house is on the market. And I hear she's gone to work up in Milwaukee for Ed Forsyth. At least they have Parker's money, but even that looks a little shaky if you ask me. Last I heard his museum building was up for sale, too."

"So you know Ed Forsyth?"

"Oh, heavens, yes. My friends and I—he was our favorite plastic surgeon until he up and left two years ago. It was an overnight thing. One day he had an office in Evanston, the next thing we knew he was in Milwaukee. I've got friends who still drive up there for treatments. He used to do my work. Very personable man."

"Do you mind if I ask what kind of surgery Forsyth did for you?" said Osborne, studying her face.

"Yes, I mind, Paul," said Beebo with a laugh. "That's one secret a girl gets to keep."

He didn't have the heart to tell her, the secret was obvious. Her smile, locked tight below those cheekbones, said it all.

"So Mary Margaret was murdered," said Beebo, waving at the waitress for a refill of her coffee. "Any idea who—"

"Who killed her? We've got a few leads but nothing conclusive yet."

"Well, those two sisters couldn't have been more different," said Beebo. "It was always Mary Margaret who was bad, bad, bad, and Joan who was good, good, good. At least to hear the mother talk. But enough of this, Paul. Let's talk about us."

Osborne gave an inward groan. This would be the hard part of the day.

"I have three lovely homes," said Beebo. "Why don't you think about visiting me this fall—I'm right on the golf course outside Scottsdale. Then I have a summer place in Lake Geneva, and of course, my home in Kenilworth. You would enjoy my friends so much. Everyone is retired. Some of the men are still on boards, of course.

"But we just have the best times together. Every day is planned. We check in by phone to see who's golfing, who's playing tennis, who's going to the theater that evening. Or an art opening. Or a dinner party. Just a wonderful life."

It sounded to Osborne like the life Mary Lee had always wanted. *Every day is planned.* Jeez Louise, is that a jail sentence or what?

He managed a smile and said, "I'll definitely give that some thought, Beebo." He checked his watch. "Oops, time for me to get going. Thank you for brunch but I have a meeting with Chief Ferris back in Loon Lake—"

"Is that Lewellyn Ferris—the woman you were with at dinner?"

"Yes, she's the head of the police department—"

"Very . . . healthy looking." The put-down was a little too obvious. Thirty years of hearing Mary Lee and her women friends snipe made it easy for Osborne to interpret her words: no makeup, no jewelry, and a sturdy, muscular frame make for "healthy looking." In Beebo's world, not a compliment.

"Outdoorsy, I imagine," said Beebo, adding, "I remember Mary Lee. She was such a lady. Wonderful sense of style."

"Yes, that was Mary Lee," said Osborne, getting to his feet with one thought in his head: How fast can I get out of here?

"Paul," said Beebo as they approached his car, "when *will* I see you again?"

Beebo's eyes searched his and he could see the loneliness. Planning every day wasn't the answer. But she was no longer the girl of his dreams.

"I'm not sure, Beebo. Life is so busy right now. But we'll stay in touch."

"I'll send you an e-mail every now and then, Paul—through your granddaughter."

"That would be nice." Looking into his rearview mirror as he drove out, he saw her waving. He felt bad.

twenty-six

Here comes the trout that must be caught with tickling.

—William Shakespeare

"How on earth did you find out about that?" Osborne heard Ray saying to Gina as he walked into the small conference room down the hall from Lew's office.

"Get outta here," said Gina, punching Ray in the arm. "C'mon, Ray. Do I ask where you catch your fish?" Seeing Osborne, she said, "Hi, Doc, I'm trying to educate our friend here to the fact that the rules of fishing apply to reporting: Never reveal the source."

Ray gave a sheepish shrug. "I get the point."

It was ten minutes after two when the four of them pulled out chairs to gather around the conference table. "Gina, you're on first," said Lew.

"You got it," said Gina. "Okay, folks—everybody ready?" Gina checked around the table, her eyes lively as she made sure she had everyone's full attention.

"To begin with, I checked all personal records available on-line relating to our three victims," she said. "Nothing earthshaking. Minor late payments on bills, no significant bank deposits or withdrawals. Chief Ferris found more documentation on Peg Garmin's inheritance when she went through the entire contents of her home today. So we know she had significant assets, but we knew that before.

"Things got more interesting when I checked into Dr. Edward Forsyth. Seems that he had at least two previous situations where patients filed medical malpractice suits and those suits were settled with no details reported to the National Practitioner Data Bank, which is a government-run facility set up as a central repository for malpractice information.

"In itself, that's not unusual," said Gina. "Hospitals have a habit of removing doctors' names from claims, which means a payment doesn't have to be reported. However, both suits were filed three years ago—during the time that Forsyth was practicing in Illinois. That helps to explain his move to Wisconsin, where he was licensed to practice almost immediately and opened the clinic in Milwaukee.

"What *is* unusual if you check his clinic Web site, is that he states he has "courtesy privileges" at the university's prestigious hospital. I checked and their surgical director said and I quote: 'He most certainly does not.' Forsyth also states that he is a clinical professor at the Wisconsin Eye and Ear Infirmary. I checked and such an infirmary doesn't exist. Fun, huh?

"However, no one other than me appears to have challenged any of that information, so Dr. Forsyth has had smooth sailing since he opened for business—until Thursday, when the tips were phoned in.

"Not only was the clinic raided this morning, but also a reporter from the Milwaukee paper called him yesterday morning to do a confrontation interview. After questioning him about the recruitment of patients who had more than one procedure done, he asked Forsyth how he was able to walk away from the Illinois lawsuits and set up a new practice in Wisconsin."

"How did Forsyth react to that?" said Lew.

"He was definitely caught by surprise. By the end of the interview, he told the reporter they could announce his retirement. Said the story would ruin him.

"Chief Ferris, no doubt that interview will make your job more difficult. When it comes to Peg Garmin, he's sure to have his guard up. You may have to go through his lawyer."

"If I have to, I will," said Lew with a shrug.

"Then . . ." Gina paused to shuffle her notes. "I decided to do some background on the Nehlsons. I found a court filing, a public record that popped up during a simple Google search if you can believe it, of Joan Nehlson's challenge to her mother's will. That was filed five months ago. She alleges her mother changed the will during a time she was suffering from dementia."

"So we have two people who might not be unhappy that Peg isn't around any longer," said Lew.

"That's how I see it," said Gina. "Joan Nehlson would be next of kin if Peg had no heirs, and Ed Forsyth would have one less lawsuit to deal with."

"One less lawsuit and two less witnesses to his recruitment of people for unnecessary surgical procedures," said Osborne.

"Ray—you're next."

"I got the photos you wanted, Chief. The prints are drying as we speak. I'm a little worried as to how good they're going to be. It's been so dry these last few days—not sure I was able to get the definition you need."

"We'll hope for the best," said Lew. "Okay, my turn."

She reached for a long, white envelope that she had set beside her notepad. "This arrived in Peg's mail today," she said as she pulled a sheet of stationery from the envelope. "It's from a young man living in Eau Claire. His name is Christopher and this letter is his answer to an invitation from his birth mother, agreeing to meet with her at her home in Loon Lake."

No one at the table said a word. Finally, Ray whispered in a voice hoarse with emotion, "When?"

"Tomorrow. He was planning to drive up tomorrow, be here by eleven. He was also planning to bring his baby daughter."

"So he *is* coming?" said Osborne and Ray simultaneously.

"Yes, I called him right after I read the letter. I told him what happened—though I made no mention of the forty-eight million dollars that he may inherit. I suggested that he come as planned and use this as an opportunity to meet his aunt and uncle and learn more about his mother's family. I'm in the process of making arrangements for everyone to meet at Peg's home tomorrow morning."

"Who is 'everyone'?" said Osborne.

"Everyone around this table, along with Christopher and the Nehlsons."

"And he knows nothing about the money," said Ray.

"No. I thought it just as well he hears about that from the lawyer handling Peg's estate. I did find a copy of her will when I went through her files this afternoon. She specifically names the young man as her heir."

"Well, this should be an interesting social gathering," said Gina with a twinkle.

"In the meantime," said Lew, "I have one problem. The Nehlsons are not answering their phone. Not even an answering machine, doggone it. So I've written them a note and, Doc, as we head out to fish this evening—if I haven't been able to reach them, we'll drive in so I can tape it to their door."

twenty-seven

*. . . until man is redeemed he will always take a fly rod too
far back . . .*

—Norman Maclean, *A River Runs Through It*

Lew pulled over to one side of the road where a sandy
patch large enough for three or four vehicles hinted of vis-
its from other fishermen. But tonight they were the first
and, Osborne hoped, the only ones to arrive.

He gazed across the road to tiny Dragon Lake. It was
just after seven and the lake glistened under the evening
sun. A cotton candy swath of cloud threw shadows of hot
pink, periwinkle, and peach across the serene surface. Lew,
hands thrust into the pockets of her green fishing shorts,
followed his gaze. Her eyes searched the air along the
shore and over the water.

"I see rises!" she said with a yelp of anticipation. Sure
enough, looking closer, Osborne could see that the lake
surface was speckled with rings radiating as fish broke the
surface to inhale unwary insects. He listened to her chortle
and smiled. Most people get upset when they see clouds of
bugs. Not fly-fishermen.

"Oh, ho, they're big enough for streamers," said Lew.
"C'mon, let's hustle on out to play with some fish."

"Lewellyn," said Osborne, reaching behind the front

seat for his waders, "I still don't believe we're here. Back at the Nehlsons', I kept expecting you to make a right turn and head down to the Forsyth place. Aren't you anxious to catch up with that guy?"

He'd held his breath as she walked across the Nehlsons' porch to tape her note on their door. Driving north, Lew had tried several times to reach them on her cell phone, but was met with nothing but ringing. Still, he expected them to be home. Home and checking their Caller ID, deliberately refusing to take her call. But he had been wrong. No one was there.

"Doc, I've said it before and I'll say it again—I've never not gotten the job done just because I took two hours to go fishing. Best way to clear my mind. Before I deal with Forsyth, I need a plan. And you know I do my best thinking on water."

"Let me help," said Osborne as Lew unlatched the back panel of her fishing truck. He yanked out a float tube while she undid lines anchoring an inflated pontoon fishing rig to the top of her truck. "How did you get that up there?" said Osborne. "You're strong, Lew, but not that strong."

"Ralph gave me a hand," she said, referring to the owner of the sporting goods shop in Loon Lake. "He wants my opinion on this single-seat float boat. I'm sure he's hoping I'll want to spend six hundred and ninety-five dollars on the damn thing. It may be easier to maneuver than that float tube of mine, but seven hundred bucks' worth?"

"You know Ralph'll make you a deal," said Osborne with a straight face.

Lew cut her eyes his way and gave him a teasing look. "You think so, huh."

She knew Osborne had no use for Ralph. He found him pretentious, overbearing, and way too interested in Lew in spite of being on his third wife. Ralph had a way of making neophytes feel they needed a graduate degree to succeed at fly-fishing, which Osborne maintained was his strategy for selling you more gear than you really needed.

"Not only is the man condescending," said Osborne after his last encounter with Ralph, "but it's a known fact that he lies—he exaggerates the size of every trout he catches by at least three inches."

Lew waded through the grassy muck at the water's edge to where Osborne was struggling into a pair of rubber fins after wedging himself, with a remarkable lack of grace, into the seat of the float tube. He had shoved everything he hoped he would need into the various pockets sewn onto the arms of the tube: two boxes of trout flies, powdered floatant for the dry flies, forceps, snips, a Ketchum release should he be so lucky as to hook a fish, sunglasses, extra leaders and tippets, water, and bug spray.

At the last minute he had remembered to slip in his birthday present from Lew: a cap light with three bulbs that clipped to the brim of his hat and threw more than enough light to tie on a trout fly in the dark.

Fins on finally, Osborne started to thread fly line onto his 5-weight 8½-foot fly rod. He was thinking over what trout fly to tie on when Lew reached for his rod and snipped off the leader. "We got largemouth bass in this lake, Doc," she said, pulling a new leader from her shirt pocket.

She gave his fly rod a critical look, then shrugged. "You

really need to consider investing in a 6-weight rod one of these days. Sage makes a nice one. Maybe a Cortland Duo reel, too. With these bigger fish, you need a heavier rod and a sinking line."

"What are you tying on there?" said Osborne.

"I'm going to give you"—Lew paused as she unwound the leader—"a nine-foot ten-pound bass leader with a weighted streamer that I call a 'tongue depressor.'" Her fingers moved fast as she tied, then licked the knot and gave it a quick pull. "There, that'll work." She handed his rod over.

Osborne followed her onto the water, kicking hard under the float tube and trying to get up some speed. Somehow it always felt like being in a nightmare: You kick hard and go nowhere. After a few minutes, he found he was moving—slow . . . but moving. Lew, meanwhile, skimmed along in the pontoon, stopping every few minutes to let him catch up. Osborne was now convinced Ralph had loaned her the stupid little boat just to make him look bad.

The water in Dragon Lake was crystal clear, making it easy to see all the structure below. They had covered a good five hundred yards and were about fifty feet off a log-strewn shore, when Lew dropped the oars on the pontoon. "You fish here, Doc," she said. "Look down." He did—into white basket-looking structures on the floor of the lake. "Bass spawning beds," said Lew. "Let's see you give that streamer a try."

Osborne raised his rod, made a roll cast, then lifted his line for the backcast.

"Wait, stop!" said Lew. "Please don't rip your line off the water like that—you'll scare every fish within a half mile."

"Sorry." He tried again, well aware that with Lew

watching he was bound to do it all wrong. He did his best to lift the line as sweetly as he could, then follow his back-cast with a power snap forward. The line pooled thirty feet out.

"O-o-kay," said Lew, a cautious tone in her voice, "think about your target. Don't just hope, Doc, *aim*. Remember—thumb covers the target." Osborne cast again. This time the fly line pooled a miserable twenty feet from the float tube.

"Ooh . . ." said Lew and had to say no more. It was bad. It was awful.

"Doc, the fish are farther out." Her voice was gentle. "Just . . . a little farther. Try again. This time retrieve on a diagonal instead of straight towards you. If you have a little more resistance, maybe you can get more power into your forward cast and get that streamer farther out."

Again a pathetic effort. Lew rowed the pontoon toward him. "It's not your fault, that leader is too long. Let's shorten it." She was right. The shortened leader made a difference. With Osborne set at last, Lew rowed off.

The minute she was far enough away not to see what he was up to, Osborne snipped off the heavy leader with the streamer, tied on a lighter leader with tippet and a favorite dry fly that he knew he could cast with significantly more success: a size 14 Royal Wulff.

No sooner did he drop that trout fly on the surface than he felt a tug. He shouted as he set the hook, then let the fish run, doing his doggone best to keep slack out of the line. Minutes flew by as he played the fish. At last he reeled it in close enough to catch sight of a rainbow trout that had to be at least fourteen inches long. So sleek and pretty! And the colors were stunning: vibrant pinks.

"Lew!" Gosh, he wanted her to see this beautiful fish, but at the same time, he didn't want to have the rainbow out of the water too long. Kicking furiously, he hollered again. Rowing his way and grinning at the excitement in his face, Lew was just ten feet from him when the fish bolted.

"Oh, darn," said Osborne. "It was a gorgeous rainbow, Lew. The largest I've ever caught."

"Good for you, Doc. All I got so far are two scrawny largemouths. Think I'll get rid of this tongue depressor and tie on a Woolly Bugger—see if it makes a difference." And off she rowed.

Osborne put in another ten minutes of casting, kicking back toward the spot where they had put in. The float tube sat low in the water and soon he found himself fighting cramps that traveled up his calves if he kicked wrong: the one drawback to fly-fishing in a float tube.

Nearing the shoreline close to where the truck was parked, he decided to set his rod down and drift. For the next thirty minutes he drifted, happy to let Lew fish the opposite shore while he faded into the landscape. He watched as the sun dropped, the water darkened, and the moon rose. He listened for the slurps of rising fish, the hoots of a great horned owl. Somewhere a rabbit screamed as it lost its head and the oboe wail of a solitary loon haunted the air. Lew drifted closer.

And so he watched as a woman with history in her face moved with silent grace under the glow of the rising full moon. Watched her turn, look back as her fly line unfurled in the long smooth loop of her backcast, then forward as she gave a power snap that sent the fly line flowing, flowing . . . to land like a whisper on the still surface.

Every so often, he heard a whoop and chortle as she set the hook. She was happy, he was happy, and all was right with the world.

The harsh ring of a cell phone punctured the serenity.

He knew that Lew had an understanding with Marlene and Fern on the switchboard: "Ladies, no calls unless a life is at risk."

Osborne kicked fast to the shore, yanked off the rubber fins, and pushed himself up and out of the float tube. He stumbled up the bank, wading boots wet and slippery on the grass, then crossed the road to the truck.

The phone had stopped ringing but its digital readout exhibited the numbers he had hoped not to see: the emergency code for the Loon Lake Police switchboard.

twenty-eight

The best fish swim near the bottom.

—John Clarke

"Go ahead and patch me through, Fern," said Lew. "I'll talk to him."

Ed Forsyth's lawyer had called three times demanding that his client be declared a "missing person." With the lawyer on the line, Lew listened in silence, then agreed to have the switchboard put out the bulletin. "I'll call you the minute we hear anything," she assured him. She gave Fern the wording for the APB and asked her to phone the county sheriff's department with the same information.

"Lots of excitement," said Osborne when she had clicked off the cell phone.

"Forsyth's lawyer is worried. Said he's been calling the lake house since late this afternoon and no answer. They'd had a conference call earlier and he felt his client sounded despondent—he's worried about suicide. He got a friend of his with a summer home in Manitowish Waters to drive over to Forsyth's place but no one was there, even though Forsyth's car was in the driveway."

"Could be at the casino," said Osborne.

"Or on his way to Canada is what I was thinking," said Lew. "Until the lawyer mentioned that Forsyth has a big new pontoon party boat. His friend who checked on the house found no sign of the boat. So he's convinced Forsyth is on the lake somewhere. I said I would check it out."

"See, I was right after all—you *will* be working tonight," said Osborne.

"Not until after we have something to eat," said Lew, slipping out of her waders. Together they packed up, working swiftly but with care as fly rods were wrapped and slipped into cases, reels and gear restowed in the correct pockets of their fishing vests. When they had finished lashing the pontoon rig back to the top of Lew's truck, she pulled out a small cooler and handed Osborne a sandwich: liverwurst on light rye with lettuce and Dijon mustard. His favorite. Also in the cooler were two bottles of water and a Ziploc of dried cranberries.

As they sat on the back bumper of the truck, wolfing their food, Lew said, "We're in luck that the worst of the Country Fest traffic is over. I told Fern to have Todd get the police boat up to the public landing on Horsehead Lake. Work our way down to Lake Alice, where the Nehlson and Forsyth homes are. No public landing on their lake, of course. Wonder who they pay off to swing that?"

"I think you're crazy, Lewellyn," said Osborne. "That's a twenty-six lake chain. We'll be there all night."

"I have no intention of checking every lake."

"Every bar and restaurant?"

"I have no intention of doing that either."

"Okay, I give up. What's the plan?"

"You know there's a lock between Lake Alice and the next lake in the chain . . ."

"Yes, but I've only been through there a few times. Why?"

"Well, I fished that chain quite often in my muskie days. I know the couple who operate the lock. We got to be

pretty good friends. Jerry, the husband, knows every good
fishing hole on the chain—though he won't tell you unless
he likes you. And Mildred, his wife, knows all the news.
All the news. If Ed Forsyth took his boat out today—Mildred will know. Chances are she may know where he went,
too."

"How on earth—"

"What do you think those old folks are doing sitting out
on their docks all day?"

The lake was calm, the moon high. A light breeze stirred
the night air as the wide-bottomed police boat sped up the
chain. Once in Lake Alice, Lew cut the inboard motor to a
slow crawl as they passed a bog behind which loomed two
dark shadows: the Forsyth and Nehlson lake houses. Only
the driveways were lit.

One large pontoon boat was moored in a shore station
next to the Nehlsons' dock. But the lawyer was right—the
shore station for Ed Forsyth's dock was empty.

The lock that linked the Pickerel chain to the series of
much smaller lakes, which included Lake Alice, looked
like a contraption left over from the logging era. Jerry and
Mildred Wright had been the caretakers for years and lived
in a modest wood frame house located about fifty yards up
from the lock. On seeing the lights of the police boat ap-
proaching, Jerry had walked down to work the lock.

"Hey, Jerry," said Lew with a wave from where she
stood behind the wheel of the boat, "is Mildred around?"

"Mi-l-l-dred," he bellowed without looking back. The
figure of a woman, backlit by warm light, appeared behind
the screen door of their house. Like her husband, Mildred
appeared to be in her mid-seventies. She wore dark slacks
and a dark sweater, which she clutched closed with both
hands.

At the sight of Lew waving, she opened the door and strolled down to the water. The full moon made it easy to see her coming. She was a tiny woman with straight gray hair cut short and tucked back behind her ears.

"Chief Ferris," said Mildred, "what brings you out so late—and in the police boat? Something serious?"

"Not sure," said Lew. She gave a quick description of the Forsyth pontoon boat and asked the couple if they were familiar with it.

"Oh yeah," said Jerry, "he came through here today with two people aboard. That's a hell of a big pontoon, too—you don't see many that big on these smaller lakes. Yep, three people. Two men and a woman. Ain't been back through. Bet they're gettin' snockered down at the Bayside—you know the bar on Little Pickerel. Doncha know they'll wake me up in the middle of the night, goddammit."

"You didn't happen to notice what the people looked like on the pontoon?"

"Oh yeah—"

But before Jerry could answer, Mildred interrupted. "It was that big blond woman who's always with him and a little guy I haven't seen before. They come through here weekends usually."

"You're sure you saw Dr. Forsyth?" said Lew.

"Sure I'm sure," said Mildred. She shook a finger as she said, "You know, I've been waiting for something to happen. I told Jerry here—those two are up to funny business. Just wait and see if I'm not right."

"Which two do you mean?" said Lew.

"The blonde and that Forsyth fella." Mildred leaned forward as she said, "They're not married, y'know. She's married to someone else. But you only ever see her with her husband at the grocery store."

"What do you mean—'funny business'?" said Lew.

"They're real cozy. I've seen that pontoon of his anchored way out and they was up to no good." By now Osborne was convinced that Mildred kept binoculars close by at all times.

"So you think they're having an affair?"

"I know funny business when I see it. Why are you looking for them—his wife find out?"

"Dr. Forsyth isn't married. I had a call from friends of his who haven't been able to reach him and are worried that he may have mechanical problems with the pontoon boat. He's been gone a good part of the day."

"Oh." Mildred's face fell. She had been counting on something juicier than mechanical problems. Then she perked up. "But why send the police out? Why not someone from the marina? He gets that boat serviced down at Luther's on Little Pickerel. Have Luther send one of his boys out."

"Good point," said Lew. "Why didn't I think of that?"

"Want us to call you if they come back through here later?" said Jerry.

"Jerry, if you don't mind, I would very much appreciate that," said Lew. She jotted her home number on the card that she handed him.

twenty-nine

*You cannot bring a hook into a fish's mouth unless there is
food on it that pleases him.*

—Juliana Berners

The sky was filled with flying saucers that Sunday morning: clouds like ivory disks with gray lids crowding one on
top of the other against a pale blue sky. That was Osborne's
first impression as he stepped out into the yard behind the
dog.

His level of guilt for leaving the black Lab alone these
last few days was so high that he turned down an invitation
to join Ray and Gina for pancakes and sautéed-in-butter
bluegills. Mike needed some undivided attention. After
twenty tosses of the saliva-slick tennis ball and twenty exuberant retrieves, Osborne did a little retrieving himself—
he crossed the road to get the Sunday paper from the
mailbox.

The air was warm under the gathering clouds, and the
wind was out of the west. Ideal conditions for fishing
muskie. And who knew? If the meeting at Peg's went
smoothly, he just might be able to get his boat on the lake
for an hour. *Every day is planned.* He remembered Beebo's
words and shivered.

Back on his porch, Osborne settled into the forest green

rattan easy chair with its matching ottoman that his daughters had given him one Father's Day. It had become his favorite spot to sit and read in the summer. But before starting the paper, he sipped from his coffee mug and closed his eyes. The effects of the extra hour he'd spent with Lew before heading home lingered. He was in the midst of replaying the intimacy that had ended their evening when the phone rang.

"Hey, Doc." Lew's voice was soft, relaxed. "What are you up to?"

"Reading the paper." He was too embarrassed to say what he had really been doing. "Yourself?"

"In the office, catching up with paperwork and getting ready for the meeting at Peg's. Just got a call from the sheriff's office. Earlier this morning two fishermen found Forsyth's pontoon beached on one of those islands at the south end of Little Pickerel. Stuck between some boulders with the ignition on and out of gas. No sign of the owner."

"Sounds like he went overboard."

"He certainly went somewhere. I called his lawyer. He's convinced Forsyth committed suicide, but I told him not to assume any such thing until we have a body. And do I have some questions for our Mrs. Nehlson when I see her."

With all the lights on and the windows opened to the warm breezes, Peg's house felt cozy in spite of a light drizzle that had started. Ray and Gina were in the kitchen, chatting in low voices as they made coffee and set out a selection of doughnuts.

Osborne leaned back against the fireplace mantel, hands in his pockets as he watched Lew pace from the living room to the screened-in porch and back again. Neither spoke. It was nearly eleven and the Nehlsons had not yet arrived, nor had Christopher.

At the sound of tires on the driveway, Lew motioned to Osborne to alert Ray and Gina. Seconds later, Parker Nehlson rounded the corner of the house. Lew opened the door before he could knock. "Joan refuses to come in," he said. "She's out in the car. Insists this kid is bogus."

"But you're here," said Lew.

"Yes, I'm here and I'm staying." He thrust his chin forward as he spoke and his fingers trembled as he took the mug of coffee offered by Gina. In his navy blue sport coat, expensive-looking tan pants, and dress shoes, he looked as if he was making an effort for the occasion.

"Good," said Lew, then beckoned Gina forward, saying, "Parker, I don't believe you've met Gina Palmer. She's an expert on computer-assisted investigative reporting who's been helping with our investigation of the murdered women."

They all turned at the sound of a light knock on the door as a tall young man with a chubby baby girl in one arm and a diaper bag in the other poked his head through the doorway. He was neatly dressed in chinos and a black Polo shirt. His light brown hair was buzz-cut, and if he hadn't had a child on his arm, Osborne would have guessed him to be a teenager.

"Hope I'm in the right place," he said, looking surprised to see so many people standing there. "I'm Christopher Glendenning—"

"You certainly are in the right place," said Lew. "I'm Chief Lewellyn Ferris, whom you spoke to on the phone. Come in, Christopher, and meet everyone."

As she introduced Ray, she made a point of saying that he had been a close friend of Peg's for years. It was during the introduction to Parker that a funny look crossed Christopher's face, but he said nothing.

"My wife isn't feeling well," said Parker as he shook Christopher's hand. "She's resting in the car and may be down in a few minutes."

"And this is my daughter, Violet," said Christopher when Lew had finished. "She's nine months old. I'm afraid my wife couldn't make it this morning. She's a nurse and they changed her shift at the last minute so she had to work today."

"Oh, your little one is so cute," said Gina, walking up with her arms out. "Can I help you with something? Hold the baby or your bag?" Christopher handed the little girl over, then spread out a baby blanket and a scattering of toys. After Gina set her down, the child, round-faced as a pumpkin, reached happily for one of her toys and shook it, her little face beaming.

"Everyone, please sit down—we have coffee and doughnuts if you're hungry," said Lew.

Christopher took a seat on the sofa next to Parker and gratefully accepted a mug of coffee from Gina. He took a sip, then gazed around the room. "So this is where my birth mother lived? On a lake?" The look on his face was one of amazement. Osborne could see that it was still sinking in that he might be the heir of a woman of property.

Half an hour later, after Lew had explained what was known up to now of the circumstances around Peg Garmin's death, Ray took over. He didn't skirt the reality of who Peg had been but he emphasized the kindness, the gentleness, of the woman who had been such a warm presence in his life.

"I wish I had had a chance to tell her that I had a good life," said Christopher. "My adoptive parents were very good to me. They were older when they got me, so they've been gone awhile. But I'm a civil engineer and I have a good job—a great family, too. Can't ask for more." He hesitated before saying, "That's what our meeting was supposed to be about today—to get to know each other . . ."

As they spoke, Osborne observed Parker. The man wasn't taking his eyes off the little one. Several times he reached down to retrieve a toy she'd thrown and set it close to her pudgy little legs. She would chortle, grab the toy, and toss it back to him. Parker would chuckle and throw it back. He was a man falling in love.

In her bright yellow sundress with appliquéd ducks along the hem, Violet seemed a placid, happy little kid. She had eyes as blue as her father's—and Parker's. A face rounder than theirs and a dusting of light brown hair.

From his chair across the room, Osborne couldn't help noticing similarities between the two men. Both had heads of an odd shape: a little large for their medium frames with round, slightly flat faces. Though Parker's hair had begun to gray along the temples, it was the same shade as Christopher's—and the baby's.

"There is one matter we haven't discussed yet," said Lew. "I told you on the phone that the copy of Peg's will that was found in her files here at her home named you as her heir. We also have copies of her correspondence with the agency that handled the adoption. But you will need legal documents, too."

"I have my letters from my birth mother and copies of what the adoption agency gave me," said Christopher, reaching for a manila file folder that he had tucked into the diaper bag. He opened the folder and looked down at the papers in front of him. Without looking up, he said in a calm, even voice, "I suppose that this will be unsettling for you, Mr. Nehlson—but you're named as my father."

Christopher turned to Parker, who was in the act of tossing a toy to the baby. Parker looked over at him and said so softly that Osborne could hardly hear him, "If they hadn't told you, I was planning to."

"You were?" said Christopher, as if he didn't quite believe what he had just heard.

"I suppose you people are surprised by that," said Parker, addressing Lew and the group. He seemed to sit taller and speak louder than he had since Osborne had met him. No one said anything to counter his statement.

"I was nineteen and engaged to be married to my wife, Joan, when I got Peg pregnant." He gave a rueful laugh. "Christopher, someday when we know each other better, I'll tell you more. But let's just say that my late mother-in-law was a woman on a mission and she was not going to see anything get in the way of our wedding. She took care of everything." His tone was bitter.

"I did not know, until after her death, that Peg had been able to find you." Parker's lips were trembling. "I'm glad she did." He gestured toward the child but didn't say more. He looked as if he would burst into tears if he did.

Lew got up from her chair and walked over to take the file from Christopher's hands. "Well, Christopher," she said, "it's time you know that your birth mother intended for you to inherit her share of the Garmin estate. Forty-eight million dollars."

Taking in the stunned expression on the young man's face, she said, "These papers are important, Christopher. They underscore your mother's intent, though you should know that her share of the estate is being contested by Joan Nehlson—her sister and this man's wife." Lew nodded toward Parker.

"Joan's challenge to her mother's will is a waste of money. It's just not reasonable," said Parker. "It'll take some time to resolve, but if you want my opinion—she has no valid claim on the money. My wife, frankly, is doing things that make no sense."

"Chief Ferris," said Gina, who had been sitting quietly beside Ray, "do you mind if I ask Mr. Nehlson a question?"

"How do you feel about that, Parker?" said Lew.

"Go right ahead. I feel like a man with no secrets for the first time in what—thirty-three years?" He looked at Christopher.

"Thirty-four," said Christopher.

"How much *do* you know about your wife's finances?"

"I think I know everything I should. We file separate tax returns because of various business interests, such as my family trust and a few investments that each of us has made, but I think I'm pretty well informed. Why?"

"Are you aware of the extent of her gambling debts?"

Parker looked taken aback. "I doubt she has any. All Joan does is play a little poker in the ladies' league on Wednesdays. I'm a regular at the casino myself. In fact, we had dinner there last night. But I arrive with a thousand bucks, and when it's gone, I'm gone. *I can assure we have no significant gambling debts.*"

"Chief Ferris has a daughter who is a CPA and is good friends from their school days with the woman who runs the business office at the casino where you and your wife play. I checked with her and was told that your wife's losses are so severe that the casino has a lien on your lake property. Did you know that?"

"No, I did not."

"How much do you know about your wife's involvement with Dr. Forsyth's clinic?"

"I know she's been handling the clinic's public relations and she has invested a significant sum of money in the clinic. But that's her investment, not mine."

"Did you know Dr. Forsyth has been accused of insurance fraud and the clinic was shut down yesterday morning? If your wife was involved with the recruitment of their patients, she may be charged with fraud as well."

Parker heaved a sigh. "Friday she learned there were problems at the clinic. She swore to me that she knew nothing about it until she heard from our lawyer. But I guess that would explain why . . ." His voice trailed off.

"Why what?" said Lew.

"Joan's been so upset the last few days. Well, I can see that my wife and I need to have a talk," said Parker. He had the look of a man resigned to a bad afternoon.

thirty

The charm of fishing is that it is the pursuit of what is elusive but attainable, a perpetual series of occasions for hope.

—Anonymous

Christopher packed up the toys and the blanket. Then, with Violet perched again on one arm, he slung the diaper bag over his shoulder and started to leave. "This has been quite a day," he said. "My wife is not going to believe it. Forty-eight million dollars?" He shook his head in disbelief. "I do wish I had met my birth mother. She sounds like a complicated, interesting woman."

"That she was," said Ray, "*and* very beautiful. So when the estate issues are settled and you own this cottage, I hope you'll let me take you fishing—we'll talk about her some more."

"I would like that," said Christopher, giving Ray a hearty handshake. "I am so glad to have met all of you." He shook hands around. When he came to Parker, the man reached to give him a clumsy hug then stepped toward the door.

"Parker," said Lew. "Don't leave quite yet. Ask Joan to wait for me, please? I need to check a few things with her."

"Will do," said Parker.

"Your wife is in that black SUV in the driveway?" said Christopher. "Should I introduce myself?"

"No!" was the chorus from all five people. He grinned and gave a wave with the diaper bag as he opened the door to follow Parker. Lew put out a hand to stop him.

"Wait," she said. "There's something you might want to have. Hold on while I get it." She ran into the second bedroom. When she came out, she was holding the box of photographs that had been under the bed. She handed it over to Christopher.

"These are Garmin family photos—including some good ones of your mother as a child. Someone needs to see that they aren't lost or destroyed. Maybe I'm doing the wrong thing giving these to you, but they may help you understand her better."

"You mean—understand why she gave me away," said Christopher. He studied the inscription on the box: PICTURES OF PEOPLE WHO HURT PEOPLE.

He looked up, puzzled, "Do I really want these?"

"She's not here to tell you herself," said Lew. "These may help."

As Lew walked with Christopher to the door, she handed Osborne an envelope. It was the envelope with the picture of the injured seven-year-old girl, the envelope with words scribbled in pencil that read "Peg O' My Heart."

While Gina picked up the coffee mugs and what remained of the doughnuts, Osborne pulled out his wallet and reached for the note with Joan's instructions to the logger. Now he knew why it had looked so familiar: The writing style was identical to the words jotted on the envelope with the photo.

Lew waited for the sound of Christopher's car pulling out. "Doc, you want to come along? Might be good to have a witness if things get tense."

"Sure," said Osborne, tucking the envelope and the note into his shirt pocket. As they rounded the corner of the house, they bumped into Parker, hanging back under the eaves and smoking a cigarette, which he tossed into the wet grass as they approached.

He gave them a sheepish look. "Bolstering myself for the rest of the day," he said. "What I really need is a stiff one."

"I can imagine," said Osborne.

A light mist hung in afternoon air. Joan, sitting in the driver's seat, lowered the window as the three of them approached.

"I refuse to give that man any credibility," she said. Her voice had the tremor of someone speaking through gritted teeth.

As Lew approached the window, Parker hung back. His head was down, studying the gravel, and he had thrust his hands deep into his pockets.

"I didn't know you were *working* for Dr. Forsyth, Joan," said Lew. "Mind if I ask when you last saw him?"

Joan turned her face away. "I'm not answering any questions without my lawyer present."

Lew nodded. "Okay," she said and started to walk away, then stopped to say, "Something else puzzles me, Joan. If I remember right, the first time we met you said you hadn't seen your sister in months—but wouldn't you have seen her at the clinic? And you left a message on her answering machine here at the house. I thought it was Peg at first, but the few times you and I have talked on the phone tipped me off. I know it was you."

Joan didn't answer. She turned the key in the ignition. "Parker! Get in."

"I suggest you get in touch with that lawyer of yours if you haven't already," said Lew.

"My lawyer is my business and I'll take care of it at my convenience."

"Tomorrow morning. Nine. My office. With or without your lawyer." said Lew, her words clipped but clear.

The Lincoln Navigator swung around and up the driveway so fast, it almost hit a woman walking on the road who watched as the car gunned its engine and drove off. She waved at Lew and Osborne to wait, then hurried down the driveway. Mild-faced and wearing glasses, she was in jeans, tennis shoes, and a light jacket. Her eyes behind the glasses were worried.

"Chief Ferris," she said, "I'm Cheryl Montgomery and I live next door. I was thinking of giving you a call. Then when I saw all the cars here today . . ." She faltered.

"It's okay, Cheryl," said Lew. "Is something wrong?"

"Well, I know that Peg was murdered and I've been worried about something I saw happen over here. She had a bad habit of not locking her doors so I took it on myself to keep an eye on her place. I worried about Peg, y'know. About ten days ago—one of the nights she stayed in town—that big car pulled in here."

"You mean the Lincoln that just drove out?"

"Yes. It was dusk and I was working in my yard." She pointed off to the right. Even though the properties were a good distance apart, it was easy to see through the birches and aspen to the front yards. "I saw that car pull up and a blond woman get out and run in. Peg wasn't home and I had never seen that car there before—so I thought it was a little strange."

"That's her sister's car," said Lew. "You never saw it here before?"

"No and I'm retired. I see just about everyone who drives down our road. But if it was her sister—that would be okay, I guess. Sorry to have bothered you." The woman started to walk away, then stopped. "Funny, I've talked to Peg so many times and she never mentioned having a sister."

"They weren't close," said Lew.

"Then why did she barge into her house like that?" said Cheryl. "She was in there a long time, too—at least an hour."

"Good question, I'll look into it."

Back in Peg's living room, Osborne pulled out Joan's note and the envelope. He set them side by side on the desk for Lew to see the similarities in the writing style. "This could be what Joan was up to the day the neighbor saw her," he said. "You remember how that envelope had been shoved between the photos?"

"And the box was only halfway stored under the bed as if someone was in a hurry," said Lew. "Someone who alleges she had minimal contact with her sister but was compelled to enter her home and leave something that could only cause pain. If I were in Peg's shoes, finding that picture would bring back awful memories. It would ruin any of the good memories she might have found in there."

"But what's the point?" said Osborne. "How would she even know if Peg was likely to look in that box given what she wrote on it?"

"Very likely she would have," said Lew. "When I was going through Peg's correspondence from the lawyer handling her mother's estate, the photos were mentioned. The lawyer said Mrs. Garmin wanted Peg to have the photos and that they had been sent under separate cover. That would have been about a month ago. Joan was copied on the letter so she would have known the box was here—somewhere. I'm sure it took her a while to find it."

"I still don't understand," said Osborne.

"Anger . . . hate . . . emotions that go all the way back to childhood," said Lew. "What I find curious is that Joan must have known Peg wouldn't be home. That may be why we have her voice on the answering machine—she was making sure her sister wasn't here."

"All she had to do was drive by Harold Westbrook's," said Osborne, "and see if there was a blue convertible parked out front. Or have her handyman George do it. His house is five minutes away."

"Speaking of George—what time is it, Doc? Let's see if that guy has Sundays off."

thirty-one

Fly fishing twists fate like a dream and, together with wilderness, makes anything possible.

—Ailm Traveler

Osborne spun the wheel on the shore station holding his fishing boat. Just as the Alumacraft hit the water, he heard the phone ring. Dashing up the walk to the porch, he reached the kitchen just as the ringing stopped. He waited to hear a message on the machine but no one spoke. Instead the phone rang again.

"Doc—"

"Yeah, Ray—was that you that just called?"

"That was Lew. She asked me to call you. They got a 911 from people down the lake from the Nehlsons. They're hearing gunfire coming from that direction. Lew's on her way and asked me to pick you up and meet at the intersection of 51 and 47. We'll decide what to do from there."

"Be ready in two minutes. Just have to pull my boat back up out of the water."

"Bring your twenty-gauge just in case."

"Got it."

So much for perfect conditions for muskie, thought Osborne, as he spun the boat back up and latched it down. He hated to take the time but the sky was dark enough that a good wind could blow up. Then he grabbed his shotgun and a box of shells: intended for grouse but enough to slow down a predator of any size.

The afternoon had ended innocently enough: George Buchholz was nowhere to be seen when he and Lew drove by his house. She decided to go home and try to get in baking the bread and cinnamon rolls that she hadn't been able to get to on Saturday. Osborne took Mike down to the lake for a swim, finished the Sunday paper, grilled himself a cheeseburger, and had the vain hope he could squeeze in some fishing.

Lew was pacing outside her police cruiser when they pulled into the parking lot of a bait shop near the highway intersection. "I have Todd and Roger going in by boat," she said, leaning into the window of Ray's truck on Osborne's side.

"One of the neighbors paddled a canoe close enough to confirm that the gunfire is definitely coming from an area near the Nehlsons' house—though it could be from Forsyth's, too. They were instructed not to get too close. I'm afraid if we take the road in, we could end up in the line of fire."

Ray had pulled out his plat book and was studying the page. "That Garmin Family Foundation property borders state land. I've hunted there. We could come in from the side along the bog and not be seen. I know a logging road that we can take in. It'll bring us alongside the property line. Be a five-minute walk at the most—and safe as hell because that's all balsam and spruce. Good cover."

"All right, Ray. Since you've been there before, I'll follow you."

The pickup rocked its way down the lane to an open area near the edge of the bog. Lew pulled up behind, jumped from her car, and opened her trunk. "I want you two wearing bulletproof vests—just in case."

Ray jumped into the bed of his truck to unlock the steel case he kept there. He pulled out his .357 magnum and a box of cartridges. He proceeded to load the gun. "You say we don't know who we're dealing with? Forsyth, maybe?"

Lew, her Sig Sauer out of its holster and ready, said, "No—for all I know, it could be some lunatics left over from the Country Fest." Osborne slipped two shells into his shotgun.

They started along the edge of the bog. Lew took the lead, Ray and Osborne behind her. The cloud cover had cleared and the summer sun was still strong in the sky. Osborne could see across the bog to the Nehlsons'. Just beyond a thicket of tag alder, they found themselves blocked by the decaying trunk of a massive white pine that had been struck by lightning. Lew and Ray circled off to the right, scrambling over the wide trunk.

To save time, Osborne went left, pushed his way through the dead branches, and hurried to catch up in the clearing on the other side. He had good footing along the edge of the bog, when suddenly he lost traction. Down, down, the water was up to his chest before his feet hit the bottom hard. Too hard—he wasn't in muck, which was strange. He held his arms high, trying to keep the shotgun from getting wet.

"Doc!" Ray stopped and turned back to help. He teetered at the edge of the bog. As Lew came up behind him, Ray put both hands back to keep her from getting closer. "Careful," he said, pointing down at his feet, "someone has been cutting along here, right through the bog. And, look—tire tracks leading right up to this point."

"Take my gun," said Osborne, edging forward toward Ray until he felt his feet begin to slip off the hard surface he was standing on. As soon as his gun was safe in Ray's hands, Osborne backed up, took a deep breath, and ducked down, his fingers reaching to define whatever it was under his feet. He came up for air. "I think I'm standing on a car."

"Give me a hand, Ray," said Lew. The logger's chain-saw and the action of the vehicle as it sank had loosened sections of the bog, making it easy to push a section off to the side.

The water of Lake Alice was crystal clear. Beneath Osborne's feet they could see the roof of a dark blue pickup. Osborne pushed at the bog and it separated enough for him to see a human arm, sleeve rolled up to its elbow, suspended in the quiet water near where the truck's window would be.

"So that's where ol' George has been sleeping," said Ray.

Though he couldn't see it, Osborne knew what they would find on the inside of that forearm: the symbol for patience, the praying mantis. "I'd just as soon not go down there again," he said, accepting a hand from Ray to hoist himself high enough to gain firm footing.

A gunshot rang out. They looked across the bog toward the Nehlsons' big house. More gunfire. "I see the shooter," said Lew. "By that tree in the yard to the rear of the house. Be very careful."

Joan Nehlson was hunkered down behind a towering basswood tree surrounded by a ring of white gravel. The tree was in the center of the long, sloping lawn, midway between the house and where the road crested to meet the driveway. From where they were crouched behind an outbuilding at the far end of the drive, Osborne could see that she was holding a revolver in both hands—aimed at the house.

As they watched, she pulled the trigger and one of the long windows along the back wall of the house shattered.

"Joan!" shouted Lew. "Hold your fire. This is Chief Ferris. Please, put down your gun."

"I can't do that," said Joan, twisting sideways to look in their direction. "Every time I move an inch, he fires at me."

"Who fires at you?"

"Parker. He's in the foyer with a deer rifle. He's trying to kill me."

"Take it easy, Joan. You'll be safe. Just put down that gun." Joan remained where she was. She did not put down her gun.

"Parker!" called Lew. "I want you to come out with your arms over your head."

"Chief Ferris?" cried a male voice through an open window in the house. "Is that you?"

"Yes. Please, Parker. Come out with your hands up."

The front door opened and Parker, wearing red plaid Bermuda shorts and a white T-shirt, took half a step out, his right arm held high. The gun in Joan's hands barked and Parker spun around, falling back into the house.

"Goddamnit, Joan—what are you doing?" said Lew.

"He was faking. I saw a gun in his left hand—he was going to shoot the minute he saw me."

"Ray," said Lew, her voice low, "think you can get into the house from the lakeside? Take Parker from there?"

"I can try." Ray ducked back around the building and dashed across the drive. A line of balsams guarded the perimeter of the long yard. Osborne could see flashes of Ray's khaki shirt as he darted along behind the trees. So could Joan. She swung to the right and, holding her revolver in both hands, leveled it at Ray.

Lew's gun flashed six times as Joan dropped. She never got a shot off.

Bleeding from his left shoulder but conscious, Parker lay where he had fallen inside the front door. Osborne grabbed towels from the nearby bathroom and applied pressure to staunch the bleeding until the EMTs arrived.

"You'll be okay, Parker," he said. "Just lie still. The bullet may have shattered some bone but it doesn't look like it hit an artery."

"She's had me trapped in here for over an hour," said Parker, wincing through his pain. "She cut the line on the house phone and took the cell phones so I couldn't call for help. Every time I tried to get out of the house, she shot at me."

Ray found two guns in the house. One was an antique deer rifle still hanging on its rack above the fireplace in the den. The other was a loaded 12-gauge shotgun that was resting on a table on the sun porch near the front door.

"Is this your shotgun, Parker?" asked Lew as they waited for the ambulance.

"No, when we got back here this afternoon, Joan had me bring it down from the upstairs den so she could polish it. Said she was planning to sell it to some woman she knew from the casino. It's always been in the gun cabinet but it belonged to Hugo," said Parker. "I'm not a hunter. I've never shot a gun in my life. I wouldn't know what to do with that thing. I—I," he stammered, "if I was going kill someone, I'd have to club them to death with a nine-iron." He gave a weak laugh.

"Ssh, that's enough now," said Lew. "No more talking until we have you fixed up."

Joan's acid yellow hair, still splayed across the white pebbles surrounding the basswood, was turning black with blood. Lew would testify at the inquest that with her deputy's life at risk, she had aimed to kill. But it was Joan's sudden movement as she took aim at Ray that may have put her in the path of the bullet that slammed into the base of her skull, killing her instantly.

Osborne turned to Lew as the ambulance carrying Parker headed back up the driveway. "Why on earth was she shooting at Ray?"

"My hunch is Joan thought we would take her word that Parker was armed and shoot him. And if we didn't, she would. Then lie and claim he had been terrorizing her so she shot in self-defense. With his prints on the shotgun, it would be easy to believe.

"But if Ray got to Parker first—we would know the truth."

thirty-two

Fish like an artist and per adventure
a good Fish may fall to your share.

—Charles Cotton, *The Compleat Angler/Part Two*

Two hours later, after the emergency room physician had cleaned the bullet wound and found no shattered bone, Parker was weak but able to talk. Lew and Osborne pulled up chairs next to his hospital bed.

"After you told me about Joan's gambling debts and the lien on the house, I decided to confront her. At first she denied it. Then I asked how involved she was with what had been going on at Ed's clinic. That's when she told me there wouldn't be a problem because Ed wasn't going to be around to tell anyone."

"And what do you think that meant?" said Lew.

"I asked her and she just gave me this look. I could be wrong," said Parker, "but I think she killed him. I'm certain she had something to do with Peg's death. She said 'I've taken care of things so I am next of kin. Mother's money is my money.' Those were her exact words."

"Well, that's one time she was telling the truth," said Lew. "Gina Palmer was able to check the phone records on your lake house phone and found that George Buchholz placed a call to your house from the pay phone at the bar the night the women were killed. Joan hired George to kill Peg and her friends and sabotage the car. When it didn't work out quite as they had planned, he was supposed to burn the car the next day but the forester found it first."

"So you talked to George?" said Parker.

"Oh no, no one's talking to George," said Lew. "About an hour after we packed you off to the emergency room, Robbie Mikkleson pulled George's truck out of the bog by your house. George was still at the wheel, and he had a check in his wallet from your wife for twenty-five thousand dollars. Payment for services rendered. He also had a bullet in the head—from the back. Same type of bullet as used in your wife's Smith and Wesson .38 revolver. His own gun was found in the cab."

"It may take six weeks for the Wausau boys to get around to it, but I'm confident we'll have a ballistics report that'll match Joan's gun to the bullet that killed George, and George's .22 Long Rifle to the bullets that killed Peg and her friends."

"What about Ed?" said Parker. "What did she—"

"That we don't know. These lakes keep their secrets. But he hasn't made any attempt to access any of his bank accounts so we have no reason to believe he's left the country."

Parker picked at lint on the hospital blanket before saying, "I told her I wanted out. I told her I wanted a divorce—that no way would I put myself in a position of being an accomplice to what she has been up to."

"Is that what set her off this afternoon?"

"That and the fact that she finally realized that Peg's will leaving everything to Christopher was a valid legal document. I saw the look in her eye today when I got into the car after seeing you people. So when I told her I wanted out of the marriage, I also said that if anything ever happened to that boy and his family—that I would point the finger at her so fast . . ." Parker shook his right index finger as if it were Joan, not Lew and Osborne, sitting at his bedside. "'You've been warned,' I said to her. 'You've been warned.'"

"What happened after that?"

"I left the house. Went for a walk in the woods, tried to get my head straight. I didn't really know what to do next but I knew I had to get out of there. Right after I got back, all hell broke loose."

Osborne reached into his shirt pocket and pulled out an envelope. He slipped out the photo of Mary Margaret at the age of seven and handed it over to Parker. "Have you seen this before?"

Parker averted his eyes. "Yes. When Joan and I were in the lawyer's office for the reading of her mother's will, she was given a letter and that picture. The letter was her mother's confession that she had covered up Hugo's abuse and this picture was proof of what Hugo had done.

"In her letter, Mrs. Garmin said that since Joan had received her inheritance already, she wanted the rest of the money to go to Peg and some to the Church. She never knew that Joan had lost all her money in the stock market. The will stunned my wife. She never expected not to inherit her mother's money.

"And the old lady's last sentence was that she wanted Joan to find a way that she and Peg could be friends."

"Orders from the grave to be sisterly," said Lew.

"Made Joan furious. She hated Peg. With all her heart she hated Peg since they were kids. Joan always felt that Peg got all the attention. That no matter how well she did in school, no matter how hard she worked to be the socialite her mother wanted, it was Peg their mother focused on. Was she up to something new and awful that would damage the family name? That was the constant refrain. When it came to Joan, her mother was always critical, always giving orders—rarely, if ever, showed her any affection. I saw it myself."

"And you had an affair with Peg. That couldn't have helped," said Osborne.

"I was stupid. It happened when Peg was home after one of her wild runaways. She was so pretty and she really came on to me . . ."

"Which is not unusual for girls who've been sexually abused as children," said Lew. "Unless they get good counseling, they're in danger of acting out. And they can be very seductive. How did Joan handle it?"

"Mrs. Garmin made me swear not to tell her. She didn't want any cloud over our wedding. Joan didn't know about the pregnancy until six months after we were married. She found out by accident when I had to sign papers for the baby to be given up for adoption. Not one of the proudest moments in my life," said Parker.

"Did you have *any* good years in your marriage?" Osborne asked the question before thinking, but Parker didn't seem to mind.

"At the time I got engaged to Joan, I thought I loved her. Of course, at that age who knows what love is. Half the reason you get married is to make your parents happy. Then Joan turned out to be . . . difficult. But I learned to put up with her. It was easier that way. My dad put up with my mother. Mrs. Garmin put up with Hugo. What can I say?"

Leaving the hospital, Lew linked an arm through Osborne's. "So sad, Doc. Old Mrs. Garmin is the one who should be held responsible. She damaged both her daughters: One she refused to protect, one she bullied. Money for both—but love? None."

thirty-three

Blessings upon all that hate contention, and love quiet-
nesse, and vertue, and Angling.

—Izaak Walton, *The Compleat Angler*

One week later, at eleven o'clock on a balmy Tuesday morning, Osborne found himself standing near the dock at Wolf Lake. Peg had been cremated, a Mass said in her honor, and Ray had just set the bronze container holding her remains in the shade of the pines protecting the bench at the end of the dock. A mother duck with ten ducklings drifted nearby, mildly interested in the proceedings.

Christopher had walked out onto the dock with his wife, Holly—a pleasant-faced young woman, tall and slim with long, straight black hair held back from her face in a barrette. Perched on Christopher's arm was Violet, who was so cute in a pink outfit with bunnies and a matching sunbonnet that Osborne couldn't help mulling over the intricacies of parental etiquette: Should he or should he not suggest to Erin and Mark that they consider having one more child?

Parker, his left arm in a sling, stood on shore next to Harold Westbrook, who looked distinguished in a dark blue pinstriped suit. Standing across from Harold was Osborne with Gina on one side and Lew, who had just arrived, on the other.

"Lew," whispered Osborne, "you got away?"

"For two hours," she whispered back. She looked more relaxed than she had in days and he knew why. The paperwork on all the arrests from Country Fest had been completed. The results from the Wausau Crime Lab had come in and they were conclusive: The tread marks on the road near the site where the women had been murdered matched the treads on George Buchholz's truck.

In return for a fly-fishing lesson, Bruce had pushed for the ballistics tests to be completed ahead of schedule. They confirmed that it was Joan Nehlson's gun that fired a bullet through the skull of a man who should have known better than to take his eye off her: George Buchholz. And it was George who had slain Peg, Donna, and Pat.

Over the weekend, two kayakers came upon Ed Forsyth, his body snagged in the branches of a white birch half-submerged along the shore of Little Pickerel Lake. A blow to the back of his head appeared to be the cause of death. However, Wausau's forensic pathologist was quick to point out that the blunt-force injury resulted in "anatomical alterations" greater than any that might be caused by falling off his boat and hitting his head on a rock or a stump.

"We figure that helping Joan get rid of Ed was the one job George had to complete before getting his check," said Lew in response to a question from Harold.

"Ed was the one who could link Joan to the insurance fraud, while George knew everything. She had to get rid of him. Hiding him in the bog might have worked, too. He had no family to worry about his disappearance. Certainly not his neighbors."

"I know where she got the idea," said Parker. "Hugo

used to have the caretakers sink scrap vehicles rather than haul them away."

"Speaking of George," said Ray, "if only Joan had called his references, she might have learned that he always did the job halfway."

Gina punched him in the arm. "Ray, it is tasteless to speak of the dead like that."

Ray wrinkled his brow to give her a puzzled look: "Really?" Gina responded with a dim eye, then grinned.

Parker seemed to enjoy their kidding around. He was in good spirits even though it would take a chunk of what remained of his grandmother's trust to pay off Joan's gambling debts. Still, he wouldn't lose the lake house. "I'll sell it and build a much smaller place on a piece of the land," he'd told Osborne earlier. "Too many memories."

He was also relieved to hear from his lawyer that the team investigating Ed Forsyth's clinic and the insurance fraud had no reason to believe that he was involved in any way, in spite of his wife's actions. But Osborne guessed that what really made him a happier man was getting to know Christopher and Holly and, especially, Violet.

"Shall we get on with this?" said Osborne with a nod to Ray. "The good ladies of St. Mary's Parish have a luncheon ready. We don't want to keep them waiting." More than fifty Loon Lake residents had attended the Mass for Peg, many of whom were hungry and waiting in the church cafeteria for their return.

Harold walked onto the dock. He held a silver scoop, which he dipped into the container holding Peg's ashes. "I shall miss her light," he said as he waved the scoop. A soft breeze out of the south carried the ashes across the water.

Christopher took the scoop from Harold. He said nothing, just smiled, as the wind caught the dust. Then it was Ray's turn.

When the container was empty, he turned to Christopher and Holly, "If it's all right with you folks, since you'll be the owners of this cottage, I'd like to contribute a white granite marker to be placed here by the shore. Peg loved to feed the ducks and the hummingbirds. She loved sitting on this bench and listening to the loons."

"We would like that," said Christopher.

Holding a sheet of paper in one hand, Ray said, "Then I'd like to read what the marker will say:

> *Here where the pines sigh to the sun*
> *Lives the spirit of one who was always*
> *A lover of soft winged things.*"

After the church luncheon, Osborne walked with Lew from St. Mary's to the courthouse. As they neared the entrance, he gathered his courage to ask her a question that had been on his mind for the last few days.

"Lewellyn," he said, "I've been thinking . . ."

"That's always dangerous, Doc," said Lew with an easy grin.

"You work so hard during the tourist season, you need a break. Gina helped me search the Internet the other day—for the best locations for bonefishing."

"Are you serious?" Lew stopped and looked up at him. "What did you find?"

"The Berry Islands in the Bahamas. I ran it by Ray, and turns out he's guided a fellow who knows the right guides to book if you want to fly-fish. Very few people know about that area, Lew. We could count on good fishing as well as peace and quiet . . . what about it? Take a week off and we'll go together?"

The perplexed look on her face caused Osborne's heart to sink. "Just one problem, Doc . . ." He held his breath.

"You will need a much heavier rod."

"I'm counting on that, Lew, but . . . do I *have* to buy it from Ralph?"

The way she laughed—he knew he could order the plane tickets.

The Loon Lake Fishing mystery series

VICTORIA HOUSTON

DEAD JITTERBUG

Hope McDonald's advice column is syndicated nationwide. So when Hope is murdered in her home, Chief Lewellyn Ferris can think of more than a few suspects. Now, she'll have to think of the perfect bait to net a cold-blooded killer.

"Victoria Houston's love for her Wisconsin setting—and her wonderful characters— is evident on every page of her fine series."
—LAURA LIPPMAN

0-425-20201-1

Catch 'em wherever books are sold or at penguin.com

Also available from
BERKLEY PRIME CRIME

Chamomile Mourning
by Laura Childs
This sweet serving of the bestselling *Tea Shop* mystery
series takes us to Charleston's Spoleto Festival, where
Theodosia Browning's Poet's Tea is forced indoors by
rain—which is the least of her problems after a local
auction house owner plummets from the balcony to
his death.

0-425-20618-1

Blondes Have More Felons
by Alesia Holliday
There's nothing like December in Florida—especially
when it's attorney December Vaughn showing a drug
company and its ruthless lawyers that some blondes
are smarter than they look.

0-425-20892-3

Final Fore
by Roberta Isleib
Cassie is steeling her nerves for the U.S. Women's
Open when a rival is poisoned. And strange e-mails
and messages prove to Cassie that competition can
truly be murder.

0-425-20896-6